VOW OF VENOM

BIANCA COLE

Vow of Venom Copyright © 2026 Bianca Cole

All Rights Reserved.
No part of this publication may be reproduced, stored, or transmitted in any form or by any means, electronic, mechanical, photocopying, recording, scanning, or otherwise without written permission from the publisher. It is illegal to copy this book, post it to a website, or distribute it by any other means without permission.

This novel is entirely a work of fiction. The names, characters and incidents portrayed in it are the work of the author's imagination. Any resemblance to actual persons, living or dead, events or localities is entirely coincidental.

Warning: the unauthorized reproduction or distribution of this copyrighted work is illegal. Criminal copyright infringement, including infringement without monetary gain, is investigated by the FBI and is punishable by up to 5 years in prison and a fine of $250,000.

Edited by: Liana Valerian

BLURB

One moment of brutal truth to my sister, and both our worlds collapsed into darkness.

The confession had barely left my lips—the truth about Hunter and me laid bare before Olivia—when men drugged us and dragged us from the masquerade's shadows. Her eyes, still wide with betrayal and shock from my revelation, were the last thing I saw before darkness claimed us both.

Now, captives in a nightmare neither of us created, Olivia and I face a twisted reality where our personal drama pales in comparison to the dangerous game surrounding us. The sister I betrayed has become my only ally in a prison designed to break us.

Hunter Reed—billionaire, secret Viper, the man who set my body and heart aflame—has transformed into something terrifying in his quest to reclaim us. We hear the men talk of how he is tearing through the city's underworld, sacrificing everything he built to find what he considers his.

As Olivia and I struggle to stay alive, bitter truths emerge from the shadows: my father's suicide was orchestrated, Olivia's engagement was strategic manipulation, and I, caught between family loyalty and passion, was always meant to be the catalyst for destruction.

With each passing hour in captivity, as Olivia processes my betrayal while fighting for our survival, I'm forced to question everything: Is Hunter fighting to save us both, or merely to possess what he claims as his own? And when forced to choose between my sister's forgiveness and Hunter's dangerous love, which path leads to salvation, and which to ruin?

PLAYLIST

"Devil in Me"— Halsey
"L0ve Like Ghosts"— Lord Huron
"I Will Follow You Into The Dark"— Death Cab for Cutie
"bellyache"— Billie Eilish
"Bloodstream"—Stateless
"Control"—Halsey
"Arsonist's Lullaby"— Hozier
"Dark Paradise"— Lana Del Rey
"Runway"— Aurora
"Save Your Tears"—The Weeknd
"CRAVE"— Beneld, Tara, Hotel Red
"obsessed"— zandros, Limi
"let me fall"— Ex Habit, bury
"Sweat On Your Skin"— Rumelis, Beneld, Omido
"I'm yours"— Isabel LaRosa
"Taste of the Divine"—Shaker, Azee, COBRA

Listen to the playlist on Spotify here

AUTHOR'S NOTE

Hello reader,

This is a warning: this is a **DARK** mafia romance, much like many of my other books, which means there are very sensitive subject matters and dark, triggering content. If you have any triggers, proceed with caution and read the warning below.

As well as a possessive, dominant anti-hero who doesn't take **no** for an answer and a lot of spicy scenes, this book also addresses sensitive subjects. A list of these can be found on my website: www.biancacoleauthor.com

If you have any triggers, then it's best to read the warnings and not proceed. However, if none of these are an issue for you, read on and enjoy this dark romance.

1

HUNTER

I push out of the back room, temples throbbing from Jax's useless lecture. Break it off with Aurora. Focus on the Vipers. The same bullshit warnings I've heard a dozen times now. The man is becoming a broken record, and my patience is wearing dangerously thin.

The masquerade ball swirls in full swing, a kaleidoscope of jewel-toned gowns and elaborate masks. I scan the crowd, searching for Aurora's dark hair. Nothing. My chest tightens. I've left her alone with no way to contact me.

I prowl through the crowd, checking each corner of the ballroom. Where the fuck is she?

That's when I spot Ari near the bar, slumped in a chair. His normally perfect posture is gone, his mask hanging awkwardly from one hand, face ashen.

"What happened?" I grip his shoulder hard.

His eyes struggle to focus. "Drugged me... something in my drink."

The words hit like a bullet. "Where's Aurora?"

"They took her." Ari's hand trembles uncontrollably as

he grabs my wrist. "Three men. Professionals. I told her to run when I realized, but I couldn't even fucking stand." His voice cracks. "I couldn't stop them."

Ice fills my veins, followed by molten rage. "When?"

"Ten minutes ago. Through the east service exit." He swallows hard. "Not just Aurora. Olivia, too."

Something violent awakens in my blood. Someone has put their hands on what is mine.

"Did you recognize them?"

"No. Black suits, earpieces. They seemed like military."

I pull out my phone, thumb an emergency code to Penn and Blaine.

"When you can stand, get to the security room," I order Ari.

Ari points weakly toward the eastern alcove. "There. That's where I last saw them."

I nod and move toward it. The alcove is tucked away from the main ballroom, partially concealed by a heavy velvet curtain. I scan the area, searching for any sign of them, any clue.

That's when I see it, glinting under the ambient light. I drop to one knee, fingers closing around the delicate diamond necklace I'd given Aurora. The tracking necklace. The fucking tracking necklace that was supposed to protect her.

"Goddamn it!" I slam my fist against the wall, earning startled glances from nearby guests. The diamonds cut into my palm as I squeeze, pain barely registering through my rage.

Jax. That manipulative bastard. His urgent "meeting" about nothing—just bullshit. All while his men were taking Aurora.

Taking what's mine.

I scan the crowded room, searching for Jax's towering figure. He's nowhere. The pounding music and laughter feel like a mockery now.

"Penn!" I bark into my comm. "Location on Jax. Now."

"Negative. He's gone dark. His security detail cleared out through the underground garage five minutes ago."

I turn to Ari, who's now attempting to stand. "Get security footage. I want every camera, every angle. And I need his current location."

"On it," Penn says.

Ari approaches me. "We need to be careful, Hunter. These men were military-grade level professionals. They knew exactly what they were doing."

I pocket the necklace, my mind already planning the violence that will follow.

Jax orchestrated all of this. He waited until tonight, when everyone would be distracted and identities concealed behind masks.

When I was blind to the real threat and kept my eyes on him.

My phone vibrates with successive messages as I stride toward the security room. Penn appears at my side, materializing from the crowd like a ghost, his eyes sharp despite the champagne I know he's been drinking all night.

"Grayson's accessing traffic cams. Blaze is getting together a team." His voice is clipped, efficient. The Playboy persona is gone, replaced by cool determination. "What do you need?"

"Everything. Now." The security room door opens before we reach it. Blaze stands in the doorway, his broad frame blocking the entrance until he recognizes us.

"Fifteen men," Blaze reports as we enter. "Two vehicles. They disabled the exterior cameras but missed one on the neighboring building." His scarred knuckles tap the screen, pointing to grainy footage of black SUVs pulling away. "I have a team of twelve ready to move."

Grayson hunches over another monitor, fingers flying across the keyboard. He doesn't look up when we enter. "I've got the vehicles heading north on Madison, then east on 63rd. Working on tracking them."

Ari enters behind us, his color returning, but his eyes still unfocused from whatever they drugged him with. "I've called our contacts in traffic control. They're redirecting the cameras."

No hesitation. No questions. Just immediate, coordinated action.

"This is Jax," I say, my voice deadly calm despite the rage boiling inside me. "He did this."

A heavy silence falls. Going against Jax means going against the Vipers themselves.

"Fuck Jax," Penn says. "Where do we start?"

"You understand what this means," I warn them. "If you help me, you're marking yourselves as targets."

Blaze snorts. "As if we'd be anywhere else."

Grayson finally looks up from his screen. "We've followed you since boarding school. That's not changing today."

Ari straightens his tie. "Our friendship existed before Jax approached us and made it something entirely different. It can exist after him."

These men—my brothers in everything but blood—stand ready to risk everything. For me.

"Then let's go get Aurora and her sister back," I say.

I check my watch. Fifteen minutes since Aurora was taken. Every second feels like a knife twisting deeper.

"I want options. Now." My voice cuts through the room

as Grayson pulls up a satellite view of the city on the main screen.

"Traffic cameras tracked them to this warehouse district," he says, zooming in on an industrial area. "But they're smart and keep avoiding major intersections."

"Fuck!" I slam my fist against the console desk, making the screens jump. "They're avoiding main streets deliberately. They know our surveillance capabilities."

Grayson types frantically. "I've got partial plates from one camera. Running them now, but they're probably stolen."

My mind races through possibilities, each worse than the last. Aurora could be anywhere. The worst part is when my mind races with all the things Jax might do to Aurora and Olivia.

"We've lost them in the industrial district," Blaze reports, pointing at four different warehouse complexes highlighted on the map. "Could be any of these locations. Or none of them."

"Split up?" Penn suggests, pulling a gun from his holster.

"No." I force my breathing to slow, channeling the rage into focus. "That's what Jax wants. Divide us, make us vulnerable." I stare at the blinking dots on the screen. "He's playing chess while we're scrambling to catch up."

"Hunter." Ari's voice is steadier now. "Jax owns properties under shell companies. We need to cross-reference—"

"He wouldn't use anything traceable back to him," I cut him off. "He's too smart for that."

My phone vibrates. Unknown number. I answer immediately, putting it on speaker.

"Hunter Reed." Jax's voice fills the room. "Seems you've lost something precious."

Every muscle in my body tenses. "If you touch her—"

"Oh, I haven't decided what to do with them yet." His chuckle sends ice through my veins. "But I'm thinking it's time you understand the price of defiance."

In the background, I hear what I've been dreading—A muffled scream. Whether it's Aurora's or not remains to be seen.

"I'm going to kill you," I say, my voice deadly calm. "Slowly."

"Perhaps. But first, you'll need to find me. And time is... limited."

The call disconnects.

"Trace?" I snap at Grayson.

"Signal bouncing between towers. He's in the city, but that's all I can tell you."

I grip the edge of the desk, knuckles white. "We need to be smarter than him. Think."

I pace the security room like a caged animal. The monitors blur before my eyes, useless without a clear direction.

"We're wasting time!" I slam my palm against the wall. "Every second we stand here is another second Jax has them."

Grayson looks up from his screen, his expression calm in a way that makes me want to put my fist through his face. "Hunter, take a breather."

"A breather?" My voice drops dangerously. "He has Aurora."

"And we won't find them by you losing your shit." Grayson stands, placing himself directly in my path. "We won't find them easily, Jax is too clever. But we will find them."

I run my hands through my hair, the urge to destroy something overwhelming. This feeling—this helplessness

—it's foreign and toxic in my blood. I don't lose control. I don't lose, period.

"He's right," Penn says. "Jax wants you unhinged. That's why he called."

Grayson places a steady hand on my shoulder. "Ten minutes. Clear your head. Think strategically. We need Hunter Reed, the calculating bastard, not Hunter Reed, the enraged boyfriend.

I take a deep breath, forcing the chaos in my mind to settle. He's right. Fuck, I hate that he's right.

"Ten minutes," I agree, my voice steadier. "Then we move, with or without a location."

I step away from the group, forcing myself to breathe. Aurora needs me to think clearly. I close my eyes, compartmentalizing the rage, the fear. I need to function like the machine I've always been.

When I open my eyes again, my mind is clearer, colder. I will find Aurora. I will kill anyone who stands in my way. But I'll do it with intelligence, not blind fury.

"Alright," I say, turning back to my men. "Let's be smarter than Jax."

2

AURORA

My head throbs with each heartbeat, a pulsing pain that drags me from unconsciousness. I try to open my eyes, but they feel glued shut, heavy, and unresponsive. Something's wrong. My thoughts swim through molasses, disconnected and slippery.

Cold seeps through my dress into my skin. Not the smooth coolness of silk sheets, but a harsh, unyielding chill. Concrete. I'm lying on concrete.

I force my eyes open, blinking against the dim light. Gray walls surround me. A concrete cell, maybe twelve feet square. A single bulb hangs from the ceiling, casting sickly yellow light that hurts my eyes.

"Liv?" My voice comes out as a croak.

She's next to me on the floor, still wearing her gown from the masquerade. Her chest rises and falls in shallow breaths, but she doesn't stir. The sequins on her dress catch the light, incongruously beautiful in this grim place.

My fingers tremble as I reach for her shoulder. "Olivia, wake up."

Nothing.

I push myself to a sitting position, fighting a wave of nausea. My head spins, and I press my palm against the floor to stay upright. What happened? Where are we?

The masquerade. Bits and pieces flash through my mind. Hunter's warning. The necklace.

Olivia's face twisted with hurt and betrayal when I told her about Hunter and me.

"I'm sorry," I whisper, though she can't hear me. "I'm so sorry."

Then I remember the rest—Ari stumbling toward us, his warning. Men in server uniforms had surrounded us. The sharp prick of a needle. Hunter's necklace fell from my throat as consciousness slipped away.

My breathing accelerates as panic claws up my chest. I scan the cell—solid door with a small window, no other openings, no furniture, nothing but concrete and the two of us in our evening gowns.

"Help!" I call, my voice breaking. "Someone help us!"

Only silence answers. I crawl to Olivia, checking her pulse. Still steady. Whatever they injected us with must be keeping her under longer.

Who took us? Why? The answer whispers through my mind: Jax. Hunter warned me about him, but I never understood the danger until now.

I drag myself up from the floor, legs wobbling. My evening gown feels like a cruel joke now, the fabric catching on the rough concrete as I move.

"Water pipes," I murmur, following the industrial piping that runs along the ceiling. The pipes disappear into the wall, thick and old with patches of rust blooming like copper flowers.

I press my palm against the wall. It's cold and damp.

The moisture seeps through my skin, chilling me to the bone. This isn't just a basement; we're deep underground. The air has that distinctive density and stillness, like being buried alive.

A small drain sits in the corner of the floor; its metal grate rusted at the edges. I kneel to examine it, noting the slight slope of the concrete toward it. My stomach turns. The floor is designed to be hosed down.

In the far corner, a metal toilet is bolted to the floor, no seat or lid, just bare steel. Next to it, a small sink with a push-button faucet that releases water for precise five-second intervals when I test it. The entire setup is minimal comfort, maximum control.

My gaze drifts upward to a ventilation shaft near the ceiling, too small for even a child to fit through, covered with a heavy metal grate secured by bolts that would require tools to remove.

The door is solid steel with a small viewing window at eye level. Through it, I glimpse a dimly lit corridor with similar doors lining the opposite wall. If the doors on the other side are anything to go by, the lock is electronic, with a keypad outside the cell.

Most disturbing of all are the two narrow cots bolted to the floor against opposite walls. They're fitted with thin vinyl mattresses and secured blankets.

"This place..." I whisper, wrapping my arms around myself. "It wasn't built for us. It was already here, waiting."

I hear a soft groan and turn to see Olivia stirring, her mascara smudged beneath her eyes. Relief floods through me despite our dire situation.

"Liv, thank god. Are you okay?"

She blinks slowly, confusion clouding her features. "Aurora? Where..." Her voice trails off as she takes in our surroundings, awareness dawning in her eyes like a terrible sunrise.

"No, no, no." Olivia scrambles to a sitting position, her designer gown pooling around her. "Where are we? What is this place?"

"I don't know," I say, trying to keep my voice steady. "We're somewhere underground. I think we were drugged at the masquerade."

Olivia's breathing accelerates, coming in short and shallow gasps. She jumps to her feet, stumbling slightly as the drugs linger in her system.

"We have to get out!" She rushes to the door, pulling frantically at the handle that doesn't budge. "Help! Someone help us!" Her fists pound against the metal, each impact echoing through our cell.

"Liv, calm down—"

"Don't tell me to calm down!" She whirls toward me. "We've been kidnapped! We're going to die in here!"

"We're not going to die," I say firmly, though I'm far from certain.

Olivia paces the perimeter, touching the walls like she might find a hidden exit. Her hands shake violently. "This is because of Hunter, isn't it? Because of what you told me?"

I swallow hard. "I think it's something bigger than that. Something to do with Jax King."

"Who?" Her voice rises an octave. "Aurora, what have you gotten us into?"

"I don't know exactly," I admit. "Hunter tried to warn me, but I didn't understand."

Olivia slides down the wall, her legs giving out. She hugs her knees to her chest, rocking slightly. "I can't be here. I can't do this." Her breathing verges on hyperventilation. "I can't breathe. I can't—"

I move to Olivia's side and place my hands on her shoulders. "Liv, look at me. Focus on my breathing." I exaggerate my breaths, slow and deep. "In... out... in... out. That's it."

Gradually, her breathing steadies as she mirrors mine. The wild panic in her eyes subsides to something more controlled.

"We're going to get through this," I say, not knowing if it's true but needing to believe it. "Hunter will find us."

His name snaps something in her. Olivia's gaze hardens. "Hunter." She pulls away from my touch. "Right. Your Hunter."

"Liv—"

"You love him." It's not a question. She remembers our conversation from the masquerade now, the one interrupted by our abduction.

I nod, not trusting my voice.

Once her breathing normalizes completely, Olivia moves to the opposite cot, putting distance between us. "I want you to stay away from me."

"We're locked in a cell together," I point out.

"Then stay on your side." Her voice is flat, empty of the hysteria from moments ago. "I don't care about Hunter, you know. I never did."

"I know."

Olivia stares at the wall. "But that's not the point. You went behind my back, Aurora. My sister."

"I tried to tell you—"

"After sneaking around!" Her hands clench into fists against her gown. "Did Ari know?"

I look up. "Ari?"

A bitter smile touches her lips. "Ironic. I've been seeing

Ari. Not that you'd notice with your head so far up Hunter's ass."

The revelation stuns me. "You and Ari?"

"Yes. I liked him before Dad forced this engagement on me."

"Wait, so let me get this straight," I say, pushing myself off the cold floor. "You like Ari. You're seeing Ari."

Olivia doesn't look at me; her gaze is fixed on some invisible point on the wall.

I throw my hands up. "Then you should be happy! If you like Ari, you're free to be with him now. And I'm in love with Hunter, so what the hell is the problem?"

"The problem?" Olivia finally turns to me, her eyes flashing. "The problem isn't who ends up with who, Aurora. It's that my own sister went behind my back. It's that you lied to my face about it. It's that you couldn't even give me the basic respect of telling me the truth."

"I tried to tell you—"

"Too little, too late." She cuts me off with a sharp gesture. "And doing it at the masquerade? Really? In public? That was your brilliant plan?"

I sink onto my cot. "I didn't know how else to do it."

"How about privately? How about weeks ago? How about before you started sleeping with my fiancé?" Her voice cracks slightly on the last word.

"You said you don't even care about Hunter," I point out.

Olivia crosses her arms over her chest. "I don't want to talk about this right now. In case you haven't noticed, we're locked in a cell, possibly about to be killed, and you're worried about justifying your affair."

"Olivia—"

"I said I don't want to talk about it right now." Her tone

leaves no room for argument. She turns her back to me, shoulders rigid with tension. I know Olivia well enough to know that she's not going to talk to me right now, so I drop it. Even so, as I gaze around our prison cell, I know she'll have to get over it sooner or later if we are going to survive this together.

3

HUNTER

I slam Kevin against the wall, my forearm crushing his windpipe. His feet dangle inches above the ground as his face rapidly turns purple.

"Where would Jax take them?" I release enough pressure to let him speak.

"I don't know." His voice comes out in a rasp.

I press harder. "Wrong answer."

Penn stands behind me, arms crossed. "He's one of Jax's closest lieutenants, Hunt. He knows."

Kevin's eyes bulge as I increase the pressure. "I swear—"

I drop him to the floor. He collapses, gasping. Before he can recover, I place my foot on his throat. "You have five seconds."

"There's a network," he chokes out. "Safe houses."

I ease up slightly. "What network?"

"Jax has properties... off book. Not in Viper records."

I exchange a look with Penn. This is news to both of us.

"How many?" I demand.

"Twenty, maybe thirty, all of them spread across the country."

"Why wasn't I informed?" I press my heel deeper.

Kevin's eyes dart between Penn and me. "Jax's orders. Said you didn't need to know."

I remove my foot but deliver a swift kick to his ribs. "Locations. Now."

While Penn restrains him, I fetch my laptop. Kevin reluctantly identifies twelve locations on a map. Properties purchased through shell companies, completely disconnected from official Viper assets.

"Why keep this from me specifically?" I ask, though I already suspect the answer.

Kevin hesitates. Blood trickles from his split lip.

"Tell him," Penn demands.

"Jax thinks you're positioning to take over," Kevin mumbles. "Has for years. Said your ambition makes you dangerous."

"And the others knew about this?" I keep my voice deadly calm.

Kevin nods. "Most senior members. We were instructed to compartmentalize information around you. Jax said it was insurance."

Ice forms in my veins as I process this information. For years, I've been the outsider in an organization I helped to build.

"When did this start?" I ask.

"After you brought in the Westcott acquisition. Jax said anyone who could orchestrate a hostile takeover that clean would eventually come for his position."

I slam my fist into the wall, leaving a dent in the plaster.

Kevin flinches.

"I never wanted his fucking position," I snarl. "Not once."

The irony burns like acid. For years, I've declined opportunities to challenge Jax's leadership. I built Reed Technologies specifically to have my own separate power base—not to threaten the Vipers hierarchy.

"You believe him?" Penn asks.

"Why wouldn't I?" I pace the room, rage building with each step. "Jax took me in when I had nothing. Taught me everything about power, control, loyalty."

Loyalty. The word tastes bitter now.

"I respected him," I continue, my voice dropping to something dangerous. "When others questioned his methods, I defended him. When opportunities came to split the organization, I refused."

Every decision I've made has been about strengthening our position, not undermining Jax. My work brought the Vipers into legitimate business spheres we would never have been able to access otherwise.

"And this is how he repays loyalty," I say, gesturing to Kevin. "With paranoia and betrayal."

Penn remains silent, watching me process this revelation. He knows me well enough to give me space.

"I built an empire that made us untouchable," I say, my voice eerily calm. "And while I was doing that, he was plotting against me."

I turn back to Kevin, who's still sitting on the floor, wary of my next move.

"Jax's paranoia will be his undoing," I say. "He made an enemy where there was none. And now he has what he always feared—me, genuinely coming for him."

I check my watch. Aurora has been missing for three hours and seventeen minutes.

"Where would he take them first?" I ask Kevin. "You may not know the exact location, but the type of property. What's his pattern?"

Kevin's eyes dart between Penn and me, desperation creeping across his face. Good. Fear makes men compliant.

"I'll ask again," I say. "Where would Jax take them first?"

When he hesitates, I calmly walk to the toolbox Penn brought in. I select a pair of pliers and test their grip.

"You have ten fingers, ten toes, and various other appendages," I explain, approaching him. "I'll remove them one by one until you give me useful information."

Kevin's face pales. "Wait—Jax usually starts at the riverside property. Old industrial building."

I place the pliers against his pinky finger. "You've already listed that one. I need something you haven't told me."

"I swear, that's his pattern! Start at the riverside, then move them within forty-eight hours."

Penn watches silently as I press the pliers into Kevin's flesh.

"Please," Kevin whimpers. "I'm telling you everything I know."

I release his finger and instead grab his hand, extending it with the palm down on the table. In one quick movement, I drive a knife through his hand, pinning it to the wood. His scream is satisfying.

"I don't have time for half-truths," I explain, watching blood pool around the blade. "Aurora has been missing for three hours and twenty-two minutes. Every minute you waste, I'll add something new to your pain."

Kevin's sobbing now. "There's—there's a basement

level at the riverside property. Not on any blueprints. Jax keeps it for special interrogations."

I twist the knife, causing him to howl.

"Continue," I say, feeling nothing but cold purpose.

"Concrete cells, soundproofed. Military-grade security. You need a retinal scan and a six-digit code to access it."

"The code?"

"Changes weekly. This week it's 391844."

I lean close to his ear. "If this information is incorrect, I'll find you again. What I'm doing now will seem merciful compared to what comes next."

I withdraw the knife from Kevin's hand and wipe the blade on his shirt sleeve. His whimpers fade into the background as my mind races through the logistics of infiltrating Jax's riverside property.

"Penn, call Blaze, and Grayson. Tell them to meet us at the southeast quadrant access point in thirty minutes. Full tactical gear."

I turn to Kevin, who's clutching his bleeding hand against his chest.

"You're coming with us."

"What? No, please—Jax will know I helped you—"

I grab his neck, squeezing enough to silence him. "You think I care about your problems? Aurora has been in Jax's hands for long enough. You're our access key."

Penn makes the calls while I force Kevin into a chair and have our medic patch his hand enough to keep him functional.

"What about Ari?" Penn asks when he returns. "Is he stable?"

"Barely. Whatever they injected him with was strong. Doctor says he'll be out of action for at least six more hours."

I check my weapons—two Glocks at my hips, tactical knife in my boot, garrote wire in my jacket pocket. The weight feels reassuring against my body.

"Ari stays under protection. When he's conscious, have him join as backup if he's able."

Kevin watches. "You know what you're doing is suicide, right? Jax has at least twenty men at that compound."

I don't bother answering. Numbers mean nothing. Strategy means everything.

"What about the girls?" Penn asks quietly. "Aurora and Olivia—what shape do you think they're in?"

Something dark twists inside me at the thought of Aurora in that basement, frightened, possibly hurt. The primal part of me wants to tear through the city with my bare hands, ripping apart anyone between us.

Instead, I force ice into my veins. Emotions are a liability now. "Jax won't harm them immediately. They're leverage. But every hour increases the risk." I check my watch again. Three hours, forty-seven minutes since Aurora vanished. "We leave in five minutes," I announce. "If Jax wants war, I'll give him extinction."

Something unfamiliar burns in my chest, spreading through my body like wildfexcruire. This isn't the usual detached calculation that I typically feel.

I close my eyes for a moment, seeing Aurora's face behind my eyelids. Her defiance when we first met on that cliff. Her reluctance turned to passion in her father's garden. Her vulnerability when I held her through the night.

My hands clench into fists, knuckles white with strain. This is beyond possession. Beyond obsession.

"Hunt, we need to move," Penn says, breaking into my thoughts.

I nod, checking my weapons one last time, but my mind remains fixated on Aurora. I've been with countless women but never felt this excruciating sense of... fear.

"I'll find you," I whisper under my breath, the promise like a prayer. "Whatever it takes."

The realization hits me with physical force, nearly staggering me where I stand. This isn't just about reclaiming something that belongs to me. This isn't about winning against Jax or proving my dominance.

I'm in love with her.

Love is a vulnerability I've spent my entire life avoiding. Love is weakness, distraction, and compromise.

Yet here I am, ready to burn down the entire organization I helped build, prepared to kill the man who mentored me—all for Aurora.

"You okay?" Penn asks, studying my face.

"No," I answer honestly, strapping on my tactical vest. "I won't be okay until she's safe."

I've never needed anyone before. Now I need Aurora like oxygen.

4

AURORA

Olivia paces our small cell, her beautiful masquerade gown dragging along the concrete floor. The silence between us feels heavier than the metal door keeping us trapped.

"Liv," I say softly. "I'm so sorry. I should have told you about Hunter from the start."

She stops pacing, her shoulders dropping as she releases a long breath. Her expression softens, the anger in her eyes fading.

"I know," she says, sitting down beside me on my cot. "I was just hurt, Aurora. Not because of Hunter—God knows I don't love him—but because we've always told each other everything."

Her hand finds mine, fingers intertwining like when we were children, making a pact to be like true sisters despite only being related through marriage.

"Remember when we promised? No secrets between sisters."

I squeeze her hand. "If that's the case, why didn't you tell me about Ari?"

Olivia's lips curve into a rueful smile. "Touché." She tucks a strand of hair behind her ear, looking down at our joined hands. "I was ashamed, I guess. Dating my fiancé's friend while being engaged to Hunter? It sounds terrible when said out loud."

"No worse than sleeping with your sister's fiancé," I reply, attempting a weak laugh that comes out more like a sob.

Olivia shakes her head. "Maybe if we'd both been honest with each other from the beginning, all of this could have been avoided."

"Or we'd still be stuck in this cell, just with fewer secrets between us."

She leans her head against my shoulder. "I'm sorry I got so angry with you. Finding out while we were being kidnapped wasn't exactly ideal timing."

"And here I thought there was a perfect moment to tell your sister you're sleeping with her fiancé."

For the first time since we woke up in this nightmare, Olivia laughs.

"We're quite the pair, aren't we?" she says.

Olivia pulls away from me, her eyes scanning our concrete prison. The cell feels smaller by the minute, the walls somehow closing in despite their solid construction.

"How are we going to get out of here, Aurora?" Olivia's voice trembles.

I run my hand along the cold wall, feeling its unyielding surface. The electronic lock on the door is far beyond our ability to tamper with. There are no external windows, no vents large enough to crawl through, nothing that offers even a hint of escape.

"I don't know," I admit. "I really don't."

Olivia's shoulder touches mine as we sit side by side.

"You mentioned this Jax person. Who is he? Why would he take us?"

I think about the brief glimpses of information Hunter shared, the genuine fear in his eyes when he mentioned Jax's name, the urgency in his voice when he told me to keep the necklace on—the necklace I lost during our abduction.

"Hunter never fully explained, but Jax King is his... boss? Leader? Something like that. They're part of an organization that requires absolute loyalty." I twist my hands in my lap. "I think Jax sees me as Hunter's weakness."

"And I'm collateral damage?" Olivia asks, a hint of her usual dry humor returning.

"I'm sorry, Liv."

She shakes her head. "Not your fault. Well, not this part anyway."

We sit in silence for a moment, the reality of our situation heavy between us.

"Do you think Hunter will come for us?" Olivia finally asks.

I think about Hunter and the way he looked at me like I belonged to him. Whatever else I might not know about him, one thing seems certain.

"Yes," I say. "Hunter will come for us. For me." I squeeze Olivia's hand. "Which means for you too."

"And if he doesn't?"

I stare at the locked door, imagining what might lie beyond it, who might eventually walk through it.

"Then I guess we wait and see what Jax wants with us."

Liv grinds her teeth, a nervous habit she's had since childhood. The sound echoes in our small cell, almost comforting in its familiarity.

"You're doing it again," I say, nudging her shoulder.

She stops, running her tongue over her teeth. "Sorry. Dad used to say I'd wear them down to nubs before I turned thirty."

"Remember when he bought you that custom night guard, and you flushed it down the toilet?"

Liv snorts. "It was hideous! Bright pink with little rhinestones that he thought made it *fashion-forward*."

"The plumber had to cut through the bathroom wall," I say, laughing despite our situation. "Derek was so mad, he grounded you for a month."

"Worth it. I looked like I had bedazzled dentures." Liv stretches her legs out, the sequins on her gown catching what little light filters into our cell. "Anyway, you're one to talk. You still do that thing where you twist your hair when you're nervous."

I realize my fingers are indeed wrapped around a strand of hair, twirling it unconsciously. "At least my habit doesn't sound like someone's using a chainsaw."

"No, yours just makes you look like you're five years old again," she retorts, but there's affection in her voice.

We sit in a moment of companionable silence before Liv suddenly chuckles.

"What's so funny?" I ask.

"Just picturing your mom's face if she could see us now. Kidnapped in evening gowns, discussing our terrible habits."

I smile, thinking of my mom's practical nature. "She'd tell us to take off our heels because they're impractical for an escape."

"And to stop wasting energy on banter when we could be planning," Liv adds, mimicking my mom's no-nonsense tone perfectly.

"She would have already MacGyvered her way out using nothing but a bobby pin and her underwire."

Liv laughs, leaning her head against mine. "I miss her."

"Me too," I whisper, appreciating this moment of normalcy amid the insanity. "But at least we have each other."

"Always," Liv agrees, squeezing my hand. "Even when you're sleeping with my fake fiancé."

I snort. "God, our family is a mess."

"Speaking of family," Liv says, straightening her shoulders. "Remember when my dad first started dating your mom? I was such a brat."

"The worst," I agree, nudging her playfully. "You hid her car keys in the fish tank."

"I maintain that was an accident."

"You were eight, not stupid."

Liv shrugs. "I was jealous. You had this amazing mom who baked cookies and taught you to paint."

"And you had Derek, who could buy the entire cookie factory and hire Picasso's ghost."

"Not the same," Liv sighs. "Your mom made our house a home. My birth mother was more interested in social climbing than raising me."

I feel a pang in my chest. Mom had treated Olivia like her own daughter from day one, despite Liv's initial resistance. "She loved you, you know. Used to tease that you were her fashion consultant in daughter form—while I was her wild artist who could never keep my hair tidy or clothes matching."

"Yeah, she used to grumble when she'd find you covered in paint with leaves in your hair," Liv laughs, then grows quiet. "I miss her every day, Aurora. Cancer is such a bitch."

"Yeah," I whisper, the familiar grief washing over me.

"Remember when she taught us self-defense in the backyard?" Liv asks.

"Dad nearly had a heart attack when he came home to find his wife teaching his daughters how to break someone's nose."

We're both laughing when a mechanical whir breaks through our moment. The electronic lock disengages with an ominous click.

The heavy door swings open, revealing a tall figure silhouetted against the harsh hallway light.

"Ladies," Jax King steps into our cell, his smile chilling as his eyes lock with mine. "I wanted to welcome you personally."

I feel my stomach twist as Jax's predatory gaze shifts from me to Olivia. His eyes travel down her body, lingering on the places where her masquerade gown clings to her curves. It's not just the way he looks at her, but the unhurried, possessive nature of his assessment that makes my skin crawl. Liv inches closer to me on the cot, a subtle movement that speaks volumes.

Jax steps further into our cell, his expensive suit a stark contrast to the bare concrete surroundings. The door remains open behind him, but the guard positioned there makes any thought of rushing past futile.

"You should settle in, ladies," Jax says, his voice smooth as glass yet sharp enough to cut. "These accommodations aren't the luxury you're accustomed to, I know, but you won't be go anywhere anytime soon."

Liv's hand finds mine, squeezing tightly.

Jax notices, dark eyes moving to our entwined hands.

"Aurora Harrison," Jax says my name like he's tasting it.

"The woman who managed what no one else could – capturing Hunter Reed's undivided attention." His gaze slides back to Liv. "And Olivia Harrison. The supposed fiancée."

Jax moves closer to Liv, who shrinks further against me. He reaches out and twirls a strand of her blonde hair between his fingers. The casual violation makes my stomach clench.

"You know," he says to Liv, "I've watched you at charity events for years. Always so polished, so perfect." His hand moves to hover near her face, not quite touching. "I wondered what was beneath that carefully constructed façade."

"Don't touch her," I snap, pulling Liv closer to me.

Jax's smile widens. "Protective. Just like your lover." He steps back, straightening his cuffs. "You should know, Hunter is tearing the city apart looking for you. It's quite entertaining to watch."

"If you hurt him—" I begin.

"You'll what?" Jax laughs, the sound bouncing off the concrete walls. "You're in no position to make threats, Ms. Harrison." His eyes drift to Olivia again. "Either of you."

Liv raises her chin, finding her courage. "Our father will notice we're missing."

"Derek Harrison," Jax nods. "Yes, I imagine he will. Though I doubt he'll look in my direction. We've had a mutually beneficial relationship for years."

He walks around our cell like he's inspecting property.

"I must say, this is fascinating," Jax continues. "Hunter Reed, the man who feels nothing for anyone, is willing to risk everything for you." He points at me, then shifts his attention back to Liv. "And you, the perfect society daughter, why didn't Hunter want you?"

His eyes linger on the neckline of Liv's gown. "Such pretty girls, both of you."

"What do you want?" I demand.

Jax adjusts his tie, moving toward the door. "In due time, Aurora. For now, I suggest you both get comfortable." He pauses in the doorway, eyes lingering on Liv's body. "We'll have plenty of time to get better acquainted."

I rise to my feet, despite Liv's warning tug on my hand. "We'll be comfortable when you let us out," I say, my voice steadier than I feel. "Whatever issue you have with Hunter, it has nothing to do with us."

Jax chuckles, the sound echoing off the concrete walls. "On the contrary, Ms. Harrison. You have everything to do with it." His eyes flick back to Liv. "Both of you."

The door slams shut with a metallic thud, the electronic lock engaging with a click that echoes through our concrete cell. Liv's hand finds mine again, her fingers trembling slightly as they intertwine with my own.

We sit in silence, the weight of Jax's visit hanging heavy in the air between us. His predatory gaze lingers like a ghost, particularly when he looks at Liv—like she's something to be consumed.

5

HUNTER

I load another magazine into my Glock, the mechanical click grounding me. The armory beneath my penthouse hums with activity as my men prepare for war.

Penn approaches, strapping a tactical vest over his chest. "I've got ten of our most loyal. They'll meet us at the rendezvous point."

"And the others?" I ask, not looking up from my weapon.

"Most are staying neutral. For now." Penn's voice hardens. "But Jax has at least thirty who'll die for him without question."

Ari steps forward. "My contacts confirm movement at the riverside property. Heavy security, rotating in pairs. Definitely not standard security."

Grayson materializes beside us. "I've disabled the main alarm system remotely. But Jax will have contingencies." He places a tablet before me showing the property's layout. "There's an access point here that's less defended."

Blaze checks the edge of his knife with his thumb. "Just

say the word, Hunt. We stick with you, not with Jax. Always have."

I study each of them—men I've known since we were boys, stealing cigarettes at boarding school. Men who built an empire alongside me. Each with their own reasons to stay loyal to the Vipers, and to Jax. Yet here they stand, choosing me.

"You understand what this means," I state rather than ask. "There's no going back. Jax won't forgive this."

Penn grins. "Fuck Jax."

"He took what's mine." My voice drops to a dangerous whisper. "I'm going to burn his world to ash."

Kevin whimpers from his chair, restrained and terrified. Grayson glances at him with detached interest. "Our ticket in is sufficiently motivated."

"Let's move out, then," I state, and all at once we mobilize.

Twenty minutes later, our convoy approaches the riverside property. The police scanner crackles with confused reports—multiple disturbances across the city, all at Viper-owned businesses. My diversion.

"Contact," Penn warns as headlights appear ahead.

The first bullet shatters our windshield. I duck instinctively as our driver swerves. Gunfire erupts between the attackers and us.

"They knew we were coming." Blaze returns fire through his window.

"Of course they did." I check my weapon. "Jax knows us too well."

We all rush out of the SUVs and fight our way through the initial wave of Jax's men, leaving bodies in our wake. Blood stains the pristine marble of the riverside property's entrance. Kevin trembles behind me, his usefulness rapidly diminishing with each passing second.

"The basement entrance is through here," he whimpers, pointing toward a reinforced door.

I grab him by the collar and drag him forward. "Your retinal scan better work."

The security panel glows green as it reads his eye, and the heavy door slides open with a hydraulic hiss, leaving us with an inner door and combination lock, which Kevin swiftly unlocks. We descend into darkness, tactical lights cutting through the gloom. The basement is a labyrinth of concrete corridors, as Kevin described.

"Left here," he directs. "Then two rights. The holding cells are at the end of that corridor."

We move fast, and I eliminate two guards who never see us coming. When we reach the supposed holding area, I kick open the door, weapon raised.

Empty. Fucking empty.

"They're not here." The words leave my mouth like poison.

Kevin's eyes widen. "But... but this is where Jax brings all his high-value targets! I swear!"

I turn to him, rage building like a physical force. "You set us up."

"No! I wouldn't! I—"

My hand wraps around his throat, cutting off his protests. "Where is she? Where the fuck is Aurora?"

"I don't know! Please! Jax must have moved them! He doesn't trust anyone with everything!"

Penn checks his tablet. "Incoming, east corridor. At least ten heat signatures."

I squeeze Kevin's throat tighter, watching his eyes bulge

with panic. A familiar sensation washes over me—the calm clarity that comes before violence.

"You've outlived your usefulness," I whisper, close enough to feel his terrified breath on my face.

Kevin struggles, clawing at my hand. "Please—I told you everything I know!"

My lips curve into a cold smile. "I believe you. That's why you're no longer necessary."

I release his throat, and Kevin gasps, relief flooding his features. That relief turns to confusion when I draw my knife from its sheath. The polished steel gleams under the harsh fluorescent lights.

"You should have chosen not to be loyal to a snake."

I drive the blade into his abdomen, angling upward to miss the ribs. The resistance of flesh giving way sends a pleasant shiver up my arm. Kevin's shocked gasp is like music—the perfect note of realization as death introduces itself.

Blood wells around the blade as I twist the knife slowly; it's warm and slick on my hand. I've always loved that initial rush—the moment when a man realizes his mortality has arrived.

"I want you to know," I whisper as I lean closer, "I'm going to enjoy this."

And I do. I carve upward with deliberate slowness, feeling each layer of tissue separate. His blood splashes across my chest, still hot.

Kevin's body convulses, a puppet with its strings tangled. I step back to watch him collapse, his insides becoming outsides. The floor beneath him turns crimson.

"Dramatic," Penn comments behind me.

I wipe the blade clean on Kevin's shirt, studying the arterial spray across the wall like abstract art. My heart beats steady and calm—killer's peace, I call it. That perfect clarity when everything else fades away.

I turn to the men behind me, blood dripping from my fingers.

"Find me another one who knows where Jax would take them. Someone higher up the chain. I'm not finished yet."

I stare at Kevin's lifeless body, the blood cooling on my hands. The familiar emptiness that follows taking a life settles over me, but something's different this time. The void feels far deeper because she's not here.

Aurora.

Her face materializes in my mind—azure eyes, dark hair, that stubborn tilt of her chin when she defies me. She's nothing like this world of blood and shadow I've built my empire on. Nothing like the death at my feet or the violence humming through my veins.

I close my eyes for a moment, and I can almost smell her—that intoxicating blend of vanilla and something uniquely her. The softness of her skin beneath my fingertips. The way she gasps my name when I push her to the edge.

"Hunt." Penn's voice cuts through my thoughts. "We need to move."

I nod mechanically, but my mind stays with Aurora. The contrast is jarring—her light against the darkness of what I just did, what I am. She's pure despite everything, an angel I somehow managed to touch without completely corrupting her.

For the first time in my life, I feel a cold finger of fear trace down my spine. Not for myself—never for myself—but for her. What Jax might do to her. How he might hurt what's mine.

I wipe Kevin's blood from my knife, jaw clenching. "I'll

find her," I whisper, more to myself than anyone else. "I don't care how many of Jax's men I have to put in the ground."

The oath settles into my bones with terrible certainty. I'll gut every fucking member of the Vipers if that's what it takes. I'll burn our organization to ashes. I'll dismantle everything we've built over the past decade.

For her. Only for her.

Aurora is the light in my otherwise black existence, and I won't let her be extinguished. Not while I still draw breath.

6

AURORA

*J*ax stands in the doorway, his imposing figure blocking the only escape route. I position myself slightly in front of Olivia, a pathetic shield considering we're both still in our ball gowns.

"I hope you ladies are settling into your new accommodation well." Jax's smile doesn't reach his eyes. He surveys our concrete prison with the pride of a hotel manager showing off a presidential suite.

"Charming place. The concrete really brings out the bleakness," I reply, keeping my voice steady despite the fear clawing up my throat.

Olivia crosses her arms. "The room service is terrible. I ordered champagne an hour ago."

I fight the urge to look at her in surprise. Even captive, Olivia maintains her socialite wit.

Jax's expression remains placid, unmoved by our attempts at bravado. He steps into the cell, and the door slides shut behind him with a hiss. My stomach drops. We're now locked in with him.

"What the hell do you want?" I demand, hands balling

into fists at my sides. "You've had us drugged, kidnapped, and thrown into a cell. At least have the decency to tell us why."

Jax tilts his head, studying me with unsettling intensity. "It's quite simple, Aurora. I want Hunter Reed's head."

The casual way he says it sends ice through my veins.

"And what better way to claim it," he continues, "than to take the perfect leverage? The woman he's supposed to marry—" he gestures to Olivia, "—and the woman he loves." His eyes fix on mine.

My breath catches. The way he says it, like he's been stalking us, makes my skin crawl.

"Hunter's been planning to overthrow me for years," Jax says, pacing the small space. "I've seen the signs for a while. He thinks I don't notice, but I see everything."

His voice rises, a manic edge creeping in. "Hunter believes he can replace me. Me! After everything I built!" He slams his fist against the wall, making us both flinch.

The sudden violence confirms what I already suspected: we're dealing with someone deeply paranoid and completely psychotic.

I study Jax's face, searching for any sign he's joking, but his expression remains deadly serious. Something doesn't add up. When he told me about Jax, he never once mentioned ambitions to overthrow him. If anything, Hunter spoke of the man with a strange mix of respect and caution.

"You're wrong," I say. "Hunter isn't plotting against you."

Jax laughs, the sound humorless. "And what would you know of our organization, little girl? Of the years I've spent watching him gather allies, position his people, build his resources?"

His eyes dart around the room as he speaks, like he's seeing invisible evidence on the bare walls. The movement strikes me as unhinged.

"You've been with him, what? A few weeks? I've known Hunter Reed for fifteen years." Jax steps closer, his breath hot on my face. "I made him what he is."

Olivia shifts behind me. I can feel her trembling.

"If Hunter wanted to take your position, he would have done it already," I counter, remembering how efficiently Hunter handles everything. "He's not exactly the patient type."

Something dangerous flickers in Jax's eyes. "You don't understand the game we play."

"It's not a game if you're the only one playing." The words slip out before I can stop them.

Jax's hand shoots out, gripping my jaw painfully. "Careful, Aurora. Your worth to me begins and ends with Hunter's attachment to you."

I hold his gaze, refusing to show fear despite my racing heart. This man isn't reasonable. He's constructed an elaborate betrayal in his mind, and nothing I say will convince him otherwise.

"Let her go," Olivia demands, her voice shaking but determined.

Jax releases me with a dismissive push. "You both better hope Hunter values you enough to come for you. Though I suspect only one of you truly matters to him."

Jax's gaze shifts to Olivia, his expression changing as he takes in her elegant silhouette still draped in the remains of her gown. Where he looked at me with calculated menace, his eyes now linger on my sister with something far more disturbing.

"You, however," he says, stepping toward Olivia, "are even more beautiful up close."

Olivia backs away until she hits the concrete wall. "Don't touch me."

Jax ignores her, reaching out to touch a strand of her blonde hair. "I've seen you at events, of course. Always on display, like the perfect little trophy."

My sister's eyes dart to mine, wide with fear.

"I always wondered why Reed would arrange an engagement with you only to chase your sister." His voice drops lower as he circles Olivia like a predator. "It's puzzling, isn't it?"

"Get away from her," I warn, moving closer.

Jax ignores me completely. "Such a waste. You're the crown jewel." His hand shoots out, wrapping around Olivia's throat. "So refined. So polished."

Olivia gasps, clawing at his fingers.

I lunge forward, grabbing his arm. "Let her go!"

Without even looking in my direction, Jax shoves me backward with his free hand. The force sends me flying across the small cell. My back slams against the opposite wall, knocking the wind from my lungs.

"What could he possibly see in you?" Jax tightens his grip on Olivia's throat while staring directly at me. "When he had this perfect, beautiful fiancée already? The one who would advance his position, secure his legacy?"

Olivia's face is turning red as she struggles to breathe.

"You're plain compared to her," Jax continues, his thumb stroking Olivia's jaw while he keeps her pinned. "Unremarkable. Yet he risked everything—his future, his position, even his life—for you."

I push myself up, ignoring the pain radiating through my back. "Let her go. Now."

Jax's lips curl into a smile that chills my blood. "Perhaps I should discover what makes the Harrison women so irresistible."

Jax finally releases his grip on Olivia's throat, and she collapses forward, gasping for air. Her hand flies to her neck, angry red marks already forming on her pale skin.

"Get the hell away from her!" I shout.

Liv scrambles backward, putting distance between herself and Jax. Her eyes are wide with terror and rage as she presses herself against the concrete wall.

"You're a psychopath," she rasps, her voice raw from being choked.

Jax watches her retreat with predatory interest. "You can struggle all you want, beautiful Olivia. But in the end, you won't be able to escape."

He adjusts his pants, and I feel sick when I notice the visible bulge there. The fact that hurting my sister sexually excites him makes my stomach turn. This man isn't just dangerous—he's depraved.

I rush to Liv's side, putting my arm around her trembling shoulders. We press ourselves against the far wall, as far from Jax as the small cell allows.

"Are you okay?" I whisper, my eyes never leaving Jax.

"Yes," she breathes quietly.

Jax backs toward the cell door, his eyes fixed on Liv the entire time. The way he looks at her makes my skin crawl—like she's prey he's saving for later.

"I'll leave you ladies to rest," he says, pressing his palm against the scanner beside the door. "We have all the time in the world to become... better acquainted, Olivia."

The door slides open with a metallic hiss.

"I look forward to discovering what those pretty lips of

yours can do," he adds with a twisted smile before stepping through the doorway.

The door slides shut with another metallic hiss, leaving Olivia and me alone in our concrete prison. For several moments, we just breathe, the silence broken only by Liv's ragged inhales as she recovers from Jax's assault.

I gently brush her hair back, examining the angry red marks on her neck. "That bastard. Are you okay?"

She nods, swallowing painfully. "I'm fine. Just... give me a minute."

I help her move to one of the cots where she sits, hands still trembling slightly. I pace in front of her, rage building with every step.

"I swear to god, Liv, I won't let him touch you again." I kneel in front of her, taking her hands in mine. "I don't care what I have to do. I'll keep you safe from him."

Olivia's gaze meets mine, and I'm surprised to see something other than fear in her eyes—calculation.

"He wants Hunter," she says, her voice still hoarse. "But he wants me too." Her fingers touch the marks on her throat. "Did you see the way he looked at me?"

"I saw," I reply, my stomach turning at the memory.

Liv's expression hardens. "We can use that."

I blink; not sure I understand what she's suggesting. "What do you mean?"

"He's fixated on me," she says, straightening her shoulders. "If I play into it—just a little—I might be able to get him to trust me. Get information. Maybe even find a way out."

"Absolutely not." I shake my head vehemently. "He's dangerous, Liv. You saw what he did just now, and that was him being... restrained."

"I'm not suggesting I actually let him..." She shivers.

"But men like him are predictable. They think with their dicks. I've been managing men's egos my entire life, Aurora. This is just a more extreme version."

"This isn't some corporate asshole or trust fund baby," I protest. "This is a psychopath who just choked you for fun."

"Which is exactly why we need every advantage." Her eyes meet mine, determined. "I can handle this. We need to be smart, not just brave."

"No." I grab Olivia's shoulders, forcing her to look at me. "I don't care what advantage it might give us. Playing into his sick fantasies is too dangerous."

Olivia's eyes remain steely. "You think I want to do this? You think I want to pretend to be interested in that monster?"

"Then don't suggest it!" My voice rises. "We'll find another way."

"What other way, Aurora?" She pulls away from my grip. "We're locked in a concrete box. The door requires palm recognition."

I pace the small cell, desperate for another solution. "Hunter will find us," I say, more to convince myself than her.

Olivia's laugh is hollow. "Hunter. The same Hunter who got us into this mess?"

"This isn't his fault—"

"Isn't it?" She touches her neck where Jax had grabbed her. "We're here because of whatever game he's playing with Jax."

I can't argue with that, though I want to defend him.

"And who's to say he's even looking?" Olivia continues softly. "Or that he can find us if he is? We don't even know where we are."

I stop pacing, staring at the unforgiving concrete walls.

Olivia's right. We have no idea where Jax has taken us. This facility could be anywhere.

Olivia stands, smoothing her ruined gown in a gesture so familiar it breaks my heart. "We need to be practical, Aurora. If Hunter comes, great. But we can't just sit here waiting to be saved."

She lifts her chin, and for a split second, something flickers in her eyes when she mentions Jax—not just fear, but something more complex. "I can handle Jax," she says. "I've dealt with powerful men my entire life."

"Not like him," I whisper. "He's different."

"I know." She looks down at her hands. "But we might not have a choice."

I hate that she might be right.

7

HUNTER

Kevin's blood still stains my hands as I slam the car door shut. The warehouse raid was a complete failure—empty cells, wasted time, and Aurora still gone.

"Where to now?" Penn asks from the driver's seat, his voice steady despite the firefight we just escaped.

I stare at my bloodied knuckles. Kevin's final gurgle replays in my mind—the look of shock when I drove my knife into his throat, twisting it as payment for his betrayal. I don't regret killing him. My only regret is that his death didn't bring me closer to finding Aurora.

"Take us to the secondary location," I command, wiping Kevin's blood on my pants. "We need to regroup."

The convoy of black SUVs peels away from the river property, headlights cutting through the night. Ari's voice crackles through the comms, confirming that Grayson and Blaze successfully escaped with minimal casualties. Two of our men are dead.

"We need better intelligence," I say. "Kevin played us. Jax knew we were coming."

"We'll find her," Penn says, eyes on the road.

"I know we will." There's no doubt in my mind. I will tear this city apart brick by brick if necessary.

I check my phone—nothing from Jax. This silence is calculated. Jax wants me to stew, to make mistakes in my desperation.

I won't give him the satisfaction.

"Contact our assets in traffic control," I tell Penn. "I want footage from every camera within ten miles of the masquerade. Facial recognition on Jax's known associates. Track all vehicles leaving the area."

My mind races through Jax's properties, his connections, his habits. I've known the man for years, yet he's maintained secrets even from me. A critical error on my part—one that Aurora is now paying for.

"And Kevin's body?" Penn asks.

"Drop it at Jax's downtown apartment. Make it messy. Send a message."

Every minute that passes is another minute Aurora is in danger. The thought of her with Jax makes my blood boil. The man has no boundaries, no code beyond his own paranoid self-preservation.

I check my weapon and reload it. "When we find him, Jax is mine."

Once we get to our secondary location, Grayson clears his throat. "Our intel was compromised." He unfolds a map marked with red dots across the city. "Jax has been operating parallel facilities unknown to the main Viper network for at least three years."

I lean forward, scanning the locations. Seven potential sites where Aurora could be held captive.

"How reliable is this information?" I demand.

"Very." Grayson slides a tablet toward me. "I've maintained my own surveillance on Jax since he executed Marcus. These properties were purchased through shell companies, but the energy consumption patterns match secure holding facilities."

Penn points to three locations in the industrial district. "These are most likely. Underground access, minimal civilian exposure, reinforced structures."

"We'll hit them all," I say, my voice a steel edge. "Simultaneously."

"We don't have the manpower," Blaze counters. "Jax's forces outnumber ours."

"Then we have to move fast between them." I look up, meeting their eyes one by one. "I won't force any of you to follow me into this. Jax will hunt down anyone who stands against him."

The room falls silent. These men are calculating odds, weighing their survival against their loyalty.

Ari speaks first. "I'm in, whatever it takes."

"I'm with you," Grayson states.

Blaze nods once, decisive. "We helped him build The Vipers. I didn't build this to bow to a paranoid tyrant."

Penn doesn't even bother with words. He simply checks his weapon and raises an eyebrow at me.

"We'll need to move quickly," I say. "Jax will be expecting us to hit the most obvious locations first."

"So, we do the unexpected," Grayson suggests.

Seven locations. Four loyal brothers-in-arms. And somewhere, Aurora waits.

I stare at the map spread across the table, each red dot representing a lifetime of careful planning, strategic alliances, and calculated violence. The Vipers—my creation as much as Jax's—a shadow empire that took fifteen years to build.

Everything I've worked for is about to burn.

When this war ends, the Vipers will collapse. Political allies will distance themselves. Business partners will vanish. The carefully constructed web of influence we've woven across this city will unravel thread by bloody thread.

My empire is about to fall, and the strangest thing is that I don't give a damn.

"Hunter?" Grayson's voice breaks through my thoughts. "Are you with us?"

I look up at the men watching me, men who've been by my side for years, who are now risking their lives because I fell for a woman I was never supposed to want.

"I'm here."

A single image burns in my mind: Aurora, her blue eyes flashing with defiance even as she surrendered to me. Aurora, who saw the monster behind my mask and didn't run. Who challenged me when others would cower.

Two weeks ago, I would have killed anyone who threatened what I'd built. I would have eliminated any vulnerability without hesitation.

Now I'm dismantling it all for her.

"You understand what this means," Blaze says quietly. "After tonight, there's no Vipers anymore. Not as we knew it."

I nod, feeling an unexpected lightness. "I know."

My phone vibrates with an incoming message from one of our surveillance teams. Another dead end. I clench my jaw but feel no panic, only cold, focused determination.

When did she become my entire world? Was it on that cliff edge, rain soaking her hair? In my office, her face flushed with desire and shame? Or against that oak tree, when she fought me and then surrendered so completely?

I don't know exactly when Aurora Harrison rewired my priorities, my very existence. But she did.

"Tell the teams to prep for the raids," I order, already moving toward the door. "We leave in twenty."

I'll tear down everything I've built with my bare hands if that's what it takes to get her back. And I won't regret a single brick.

8

AURORA

I drift in and out of a heavy sleep, my limbs feeling like they're filled with cement. Something's wrong. The soup. The soup they brought us earlier—it tasted bitter. I didn't finish mine, but I had enough.

A metallic click pierces my consciousness. The cell door.

I try to open my eyes fully, but my lids feel weighted. The fluorescent light above burns into my retinas through the sliver I manage. My heart races while my body refuses to respond.

Footsteps. Confident, measured steps approaching our cots.

I strain to turn my head, the simple movement requiring monumental effort. My neck muscles barely respond, allowing just enough rotation to see the outline of a man standing over Olivia's cot.

Jax.

His broad shoulders and imposing stance are unmistakable even in my compromised state. Why can't I move? The panic rises in my chest like floodwater, but my limbs remain unresponsive.

"Miss Harrison," Jax's voice is smooth, controlled. "I hope you found the accommodations acceptable."

To my horror, Olivia sits up with ease. Her movements are normal, fluid. She wasn't affected. Did she not eat the soup? Or was mine specifically targeted?

"As acceptable as a prison cell can be," Liv responds.

I try desperately to call out, to warn her, to do anything. My mouth won't form words—just a slight moan escapes my throat. Neither of them notices.

My sister stands now, facing Jax directly. She doesn't appear drugged at all.

I fight against whatever is paralyzing me, willing my fingers to twitch, my legs to move. Nothing responds. I'm trapped inside my own body, forced to watch as Jax moves closer to Olivia.

The helplessness is suffocating. My sister is standing there, vulnerable, while I lie here useless. What did they put in my food? Why am I the only one affected?

Jax closes the distance between himself and Liv in two long strides. Before she can back away, his hand shoots out, fingers wrapping around the back of her neck.

"You have your father's pride," he says, voice dropping to a dangerous purr. "But in a much prettier packaging."

I try to scream, but my throat produces only a pathetic whimper. The drug pulses through my system, leaving me conscious but useless.

Jax's fingers tighten on her neck, not enough to choke but enough to control. His thumb traces small circles on her skin. The gesture looks almost tender, making it more revolting.

"Let go of me," Liv demands.

Jax leans closer, his face inches from hers. His gaze roams over her features, lingering on her lips, then her throat, then lower. Not like he's admiring her, but like he's cataloging parts of a meal.

"I wonder what Reed sees in your sister that he doesn't see in you," Jax murmurs, his eyes flicking briefly toward my paralyzed form before returning to Liv.

I struggle against the chemical prison of my body as Jax's grip on my sister's neck tightens.

"Such a waste," he breathes, his free hand rising to hover near her face. "Hunter had you all wrapped up like a present he never intended to unwrap."

Liv tries to pull away, but his grip holds her firmly. "Don't touch me."

The corner of his mouth lifts in a cruel smile. "Your sister seems to enjoy being touched." His eyes flick toward me. "Don't you, Aurora?"

My fingers twitch—the most movement I can manage. A small victory lost in the horror unfolding before me.

"I bet you're responsive," Jax continues, his attention back on Liv. His hand moves to her collarbone, fingers tracing the exposed skin above her gown's neckline. "I've been watching you since Hunter arranged your engagement. The way you move. The way you tilt your head when you laugh."

His palm slides lower, cupping her breast through the fabric of her dress. Liv's face freezes in shock, but he doesn't release her.

"I could make you forget all about any other man," he whispers. "Show you what it's like to be with someone who knows exactly what this perfect body needs."

I manage to push a ragged sound from my throat. Useless. Pathetic.

Jax's thumb circles over the peak of Olivia's breast as he leans closer. "I bet you get wet when a man takes control.

When he tells you exactly what he's going to do to that tight little—"

"Get your hands off me," Olivia spits, her voice trembling with rage rather than fear.

His smile widens, seemingly pleased by her defiance. "The things I could do to that mouth," he murmurs. "The ways I could make you beg."

I try to scream as Jax's hand shoots out and grabs Olivia's wrist. Her eyes widen as he forces her palm against the front of his suit pants. My stomach lurches as I realize he's hard, the outline clearly visible even from where I lie paralyzed.

"Feel what you do to me," he growls.

What happens next makes my blood run cold. Olivia makes a small sound in her throat—a soft mewl that doesn't sound entirely like protest. Is it closer to... pleasure? The noise is brief, barely audible, but unmistakable.

No. This can't be happening. My mind rejects what my ears just heard.

Olivia's cheeks flush deep crimson. She looks mortified, as if her body has betrayed her. She tries to jerk her hand away, but Jax holds it firmly in place.

"Stop," she whispers, but the command lacks the conviction of her earlier defiance.

Jax laughs—a deep, knowing sound that echoes off the concrete walls. His eyes gleam with predatory satisfaction.

"I knew it," he says, his voice dropping an octave lower. "You're a dirty girl beneath all that proper society polish, aren't you?" He leans in closer, his lips nearly brushing her ear. "Just gagging to get a real fucking by a man like me."

The drugs in my system prevent me from vomiting, but bile rises in my throat anyway. I manage to twitch my fingers against the thin mattress of the cot, but nothing more. Helpless tears leak from the corners of my eyes.

Olivia stands frozen, her hand trapped against his erection, her face a mask of confusion and shame.

"Feel how big I am," Jax commands, his voice rumbling through the cell. "Go on. Feel what a real man is like."

I fight against the paralyzing agent in my system, desperate to scream, to move, to do anything. But I can only watch as my sister's slender fingers wrap around his length through his pants.

To my shock, Olivia squeezes him, her hand sliding along what's clearly far larger than I would have expected. Her movement isn't tentative—it's deliberate, almost sensual.

Is this the plan she mentioned? Playing seductress to gain his trust? Or is this something else entirely? The uncertainty churns my already nauseated stomach.

"That's it," Jax purrs, his eyes half-lidded with pleasure. "Good girl."

The praise drips from his lips like poison honey. I try to convince myself Liv's playing a dangerous game—that this is all strategic. But the flush spreading across her cheeks tells a different story.

Olivia's tongue darts out, moistening her lips in a gesture that looks disturbingly genuine. Her breathing has quickened, her chest rising and falling rapidly against the bodice of her gown.

Jax's free hand catches her chin, forcing her to look up at him. "You know what's funny?" he asks, thumb brushing across her bottom lip. "The only man who can make you see fucking stars isn't some corporate pretty boy. It's a villain."

His words hang in the air between them. Olivia doesn't pull away.

"I can sense it," he continues, voice dropping to a seductive rumble. "You've always craved a villain like me. Someone who understands the darkness." His fingers tighten on her jaw. "Someone who doesn't just peek into the abyss, but lives in it."

My tears flow freely now, sliding down my cheek into my hair.

Jax's hand slides up Olivia's thigh, disappearing beneath the fabric of her gown. My sister's eyes flutter, her lips parting. His movements are slow, deliberate, as if he's savoring it.

"Let's see how the princess really feels about the monster," he murmurs, his fingers traveling higher.

I'm screaming inside my immobilized body. This can't be happening. Not to Liv. Not while I'm lying here unable to help her.

Jax's expression changes suddenly—his eyes widening slightly before darkening with unmistakable lust. "Fuck," he growls. "You're soaked."

The predatory smile that spreads across his face makes my soul shrivel. His fingers are clearly moving beneath her dress now, and Liv's breathing has become shallow, uneven.

What terrifies me most is that my sister's hand remains firmly on the bulge in his pants. Her fingers continue to squeeze and stroke his length through the fabric. Her eyes hold a mixture of shame and arousal that I can't comprehend.

"You're so fucking dirty," Jax says, his voice thick with desire. "Getting wet for the man holding you captive." His gaze rakes over her flushed face. "While desperately clinging to my cock."

Olivia's lips tremble, but she doesn't pull away. Her fingers tighten around him, a gesture that seems to please him immensely.

The paralytic drug keeps me immobile and powerless. I can't save my sister from this monster. I can't even save myself. All I can do is pray that Hunter finds us before something truly unforgivable happens.

9

HUNTER

Blood drips from the combat knife in my hand as I step over the body of Jax's guard. He won't be the last to die tonight. Not by a long shot.

"Clear," Penn whispers through the comm in my ear. "East wing secure."

"South entrance locked down," Grayson confirms. "Two guys neutralized."

The abandoned pharmaceutical facility looms around us; a labyrinth of darkened corridors and equipment left to rust. Moonlight filters through broken windows, casting long shadows across concrete floors. The air reeks of chemicals and neglect.

"Movement ahead," I murmur, signaling my team to halt.

The red dot from my laser sight dances across the darkness. Something glints in the corridor ahead—a thin wire stretched ankle-high across our path.

"Trip wire," I gesture, dropping to one knee.

Blaze kneels beside me, his expression grim. "This isn't random. They knew we'd come."

The realization burns through me, icy and precise. Jax has been planning this war longer than I suspected. Each of these locations is a carefully constructed death trap.

I clip the wire with specialized cutters, the tension releasing with a soft ping. Behind it, pressure pads line the floor in a staggered pattern.

"They're herding us," Penn observes. "Forcing a specific path."

"Straight into an ambush," I finish for him, tasting copper on my tongue.

Somewhere in this city, Aurora is being held by a man who's had years to plan my downfall. The thought of her in Jax's hands sharpens my focus to a lethal point.

"Blaze, bypass the corridor. Create our own entry point through the east lab. Grayson, deploy thermal imaging. I need heat signatures before we breach."

They do as I instruct, even as I catch the unspoken concern in their eyes. We've hit two locations already with no sign of Aurora or Olivia.

"Hunt," Grayson's voice crackles through my earpiece. "Thermal's showing multiple heat sources in the sub-basement. Could be targets, could be a trap."

"Could be both," I respond, checking my weapon.

The rage I've kept contained since Aurora's abduction simmers just beneath my skin. If she's here, nothing will stop me from reaching her. If she's not, I'll tear through every one of Jax's men until I find where he's hiding her.

We breach the sub-basement with explosive precision, simultaneously through four entry points. The moment we clear the doorways, gunfire erupts.

"Take cover!" Penn shouts as bullets chip concrete inches from his head.

I pivot and put two rounds through a gunman's throat

before he can adjust his aim. Blood sprays across industrial piping as he drops. Three men appear from behind chemical tanks, firing modified carbines.

"Cover me!" I command, breaking left while Blaze lays down suppressing fire.

The weight of my rage propels me forward, each movement calculated and deadly. I slide behind a concrete pillar as rounds impact where I stood moments before. Without hesitation, I swing around the opposite side and eliminate two more of Jax's men with mechanical efficiency.

"Hunter, your three o'clock!" Grayson warns.

I drop to one knee and fire upward, catching the fourth gunman as he attempts to flank from an elevated platform. His body crashes onto the equipment below.

"Clear this level!" I order, advancing through the space. "Find me something!"

They sweep each room, neutralizing resistance. Bodies of Jax's men litter the facility, but something feels wrong.

"Hunter," Blaze calls, his voice tight. "This room's been staged."

I join him in what appears to be a holding cell. Two chairs sit in the center, restraints hanging loose. A discarded black evening gown—identical to the one Aurora wore—lies crumpled in the corner.

"It's theater," I snarl, kicking one of the chairs across the room. "They were never here."

"Boss." Grayson's voice comes through my comm. "Security office, northeast corner. You need to see this."

I find him staring at a monitor, its blue light reflecting off his grim expression. On screen, Jax King smiles directly into the camera.

"Hello, Hunter," he says, looking amused. "Enjoying our little game of hide and seek? I've left breadcrumbs at each location. Some might call it a wild goose chase, but I prefer to think of it as... foreplay."

Behind him, I glimpse a wall I recognize from another facility.

"He's been recording these in advance," Grayson says. "Leading us exactly where he wants us to go."

I stare at Jax's smug face on the monitor, everything clicking into place. The trip wires. The breadcrumbs. The staged cells. The perfectly timed video messages.

"He's playing with us," I say, my voice unnaturally calm. "This isn't about eliminating a threat—it's about breaking me first."

Penn exchanges glances with Grayson. "Hunter—"

"We need to regroup," I cut him off, turning away from the screen. "This is the third location tonight. Three more failures and we're no closer to finding them."

Something inside me fractures.

With a primal sound that barely resembles a human voice, I slam my fist into the concrete. Pain explodes through my hand, bright and clarifying. I hit it again. And again. Blood smears across the gray surface as my knuckles split open.

I welcome the agony, relish it. Each impact sends shocks of pain through my arm, cutting through the fog of rage and fear clouding my mind. The physical suffering anchors me to reality when nothing else can.

Blood drips between my fingers, pooling on the floor. I breathe heavily, finding strange comfort in my self-destruction.

This is what Jax doesn't understand. Pain doesn't break me—it focuses me.

10

AURORA

The concrete walls feel closer now than when we arrived, our prison shrinking with each passing hour. We've been taken out one by one to shower and returned immediately after. And they've given us a fresh nightgown. I've regained control of my limbs since the drugging incident, but being able to move freely in a locked cell feels like its own special torture.

"Water delivery," a guard announces, sliding two bottles through the meal slot. The routine never changes—breakfast at seven, water at ten and three, dinner at six. Like clockwork in hell.

Olivia sits on her cot, knees pulled to her chest. She hasn't met my eyes properly since that night. Since what Jax did. Since what I saw.

"Liv," I say softly. "You need to drink something."

She shakes her head almost imperceptibly. Dark circles rim her eyes, her once-perfect blonde hair hanging limply around her face.

The electronic lock disengages with its familiar

mechanical whine. My stomach tightens instantly—it's not a scheduled mealtime. That means only one thing.

Jax enters, immaculate as always in a black tailored suit. Two-armed guards flank the doorway behind him.

"Good morning, ladies." His voice carries that unsettling blend of politeness and menace. "Day five of our little arrangement. How are we feeling?"

Neither of us responds. I've learned that silence infuriates him more than defiance.

"Not talkative today?" He crosses to Liv's cot, standing too close. "That's a shame. I so enjoy our conversations."

Liv shrinks further into herself. I catch her trembling.

"Perhaps Aurora would like to chat instead?" He turns his dark gaze to me. "Tell me, what's your favorite childhood memory with your sister? Before she became such a willing—"

"Stop it," I snap, unable to contain myself.

He smiles, victorious at getting a reaction. "Protective, aren't we? Though I wonder why. Your sister seems quite capable of making her own... decisions."

Olivia makes a small sound—something between a whimper and a sob.

"Leave her alone," I say, standing despite every instinct screaming to appear smaller, less threatening.

Jax ignores me, reaching to brush a strand of hair from Olivia's face. She flinches but doesn't pull away. The shame in her eyes when she finally glances at me is unbearable.

"Such lovely sisters," Jax murmurs, his fingers trailing down to Olivia's neck. "So different, yet equally... entertaining."

Jax's fingers slide from Olivia's neck to her jaw, forcing her head up. "Drink," he commands, grabbing one of the water bottles and pressing it against her lips.

Olivia clamps her mouth shut, turning her face away.

"I said drink." His voice drops an octave, that dangerous edge returning. With one hand, he pinches her nose closed while the other tips the bottle to her lips.

Olivia struggles briefly but can't break his grip. When she finally gasps for air, water floods her mouth. She chokes, coughs, but Jax doesn't relent until half the bottle is empty, water spilling down her chin and neck, darkening the nightgown.

My stomach churns. I've already finished my water—downed it mindlessly minutes before Jax arrived. What's in it?

"Perfect. Now we're ready for our entertainment." Jax releases Olivia, who collapses into a coughing fit. He pulls a tablet from his jacket pocket and positions it so we can both see.

The screen lights up with a news channel logo. The headline scrolls across the bottom.

TECH MOGUL HUNTER REED LINKED TO ORGANIZED CRIME SYNDICATE.

"Your boyfriend's quite the celebrity these days," Jax says, his eyes fixed on my reaction.

The footage shows Hunter leaving a building, his expression cold as reporters shout questions.

"This carefully edited garbage doesn't prove anything," I say.

Jax laughs. "The public disagrees. Your Hunter is officially Public Enemy Number One. I doubt he has time to even look for you."

My heart sinks despite myself.

"Five days," Jax continues. "I expected him sooner. Perhaps you're not as important to him as you believed?"

He studies my face with clinical interest. "Or maybe he's simply outmatched this time."

I watch the screen, the images of Hunter burning into my mind. Five days. Has it really been that long? The seed of doubt takes root despite my determination to crush it. What if Hunter can't find us? What if Jax has outmaneuvered him?

"You look troubled, Aurora," Jax says, putting the tablet away. "Having second thoughts about your knight in crime-stained armor?"

I don't answer, but my silence feels more like weakness than defiance now.

Jax turns his attention back to Olivia. "Your sister still believes in fairy tales." His hand slides to her shoulder, fingers tracing her collarbone. "You're more practical, aren't you, Liv?"

To my horror, Liv doesn't pull away. Her eyes remain downcast, but she leans into his touch.

"That's better," Jax murmurs. His hand moves lower, tracing the outline of her breast through the fabric of her nightgown.

"Liv," I whisper, my voice catching.

Jax's other hand cups Liv's face. "Tell your sister how you feel when I touch you."

Liv's eyes flick to mine, a flash of something—shame? Fear? Something else? —before dropping again.

When Jax guides her hand to the front of his trousers, she doesn't resist.

My stomach churns. "What did you put in the water?" I demand suddenly.

Jax turns to me, smiling while his hand remains on Olivia's. "Just something to help you both sleep deeply. Very deeply."

The implication hits me like ice water. Sleep deeply—deeply enough that we wouldn't know if he came in during the night. Wouldn't know what he did to us while we were unconscious.

"You drugged me again?"

"Consider it a courtesy," Jax replies smoothly. "The human mind needs rest, especially in stressful circumstances."

"You're a monster," I whisper.

"I never claimed to be anything but a monster, Aurora." Jax's voice carries no shame. "Your mistake was assuming your Hunter is any different."

He turns back to Liv, his fingers threading through her blonde hair, tilting her head to expose the pale curve of her neck. When his lips touch her skin, my stomach twists into a knot of revulsion.

But what happens next freezes my blood.

Liv moans.

Not a whimper of fear or a cry of distress, but a sound I recognize from my own sounds I make with Hunter—pleasure. Her eyes flutter closed, body arching toward Jax as his mouth works its way down her throat.

Is this real? My mind races through possibilities. Is Liv playing him—pretending to respond to gain his trust? It would align with the strategy she mentioned days ago, using his attraction to find an escape opportunity.

But the flush spreading across her cheeks looks genuine. The way her fingers curl into the fabric of his suit jacket seems instinctive. She's either a very good fucking actress or...

I search her face for some sign—a flicker of revulsion behind her eyelids, a moment of eye contact to reassure me this is all an act—but find nothing. If she's playing a role, she's committed to it completely.

Or maybe...maybe she truly responds to him. Stockholm syndrome? The drugs in our water? Or a darkness in my sister I've never recognized before?

I want to scream, to pull her away from him, but I'm frozen in place, watching this nightmare unfold with no way to determine if my sister is a victim or a willing participant in her own corruption.

Jax's hand slides up along her thigh. The sight makes me physically ill. He leans in, his lips brushing against her ear, but his eyes remain fixed on me—watching my reaction.

"Tonight," he whispers, loud enough for me to hear every syllable, "when the drugs take effect, and you're deep asleep, I'm going to come back in here and eat your perfect little pussy until you come in your sleep. Would you like that, Olivia?"

"Fuck off," I spit, lunging forward before remembering the armed guards at the door. "Don't even think about touching her, you psychopath."

Liv's reaction stops me cold. Instead of revulsion or fear, her pupils dilate, lips parting slightly. A flush creeps up her neck as she gazes at Jax through half-lidded eyes. She looks... aroused.

Who is this woman? The sister I grew up with, shared secrets with, comforted through breakups, and celebrated achievements with—she's become a stranger in five days. Or maybe she was always a stranger, and I just never saw it.

Liv suddenly reaches up, grabs Jax's face between her hands, and crushes her lips against his. The move clearly takes him by surprise—his eyes widen before he recovers, gripping her waist and deepening the kiss.

"What the fuck, Liv?" I gasp, unable to process what I'm seeing. "What about Ari?"

Jax immediately stiffens, breaking away from Olivia. His hand remains possessively on her thigh.

"Ari?" His voice drops dangerously. "What do you mean?"

The temperature in the room seems to plummet. I realize I've said something significant, something that matters to Jax in ways I don't understand. But I press forward, desperate for any advantage.

"She was dating Ari. Ari Carter. Before all this."

Jax's eyes darken as he turns to Liv. "Is that what you like? A nice pretty boy who would look perfect on his hands and knees sucking cock?" He grabs her chin roughly. "Not a real man?"

Liv bites her lip. "No," she whispers, her voice breathy. "I don't want a boy. I like you." She leans forward and kisses him again, her hands sliding up his chest.

My stomach turns as I watch my sister press against this monster, her body language broadcasting desire rather than revulsion. This can't be happening.

Jax pulls back, a satisfied smirk spreading across his face as he strokes her cheek. "Good girl," he murmurs, his thumb brushing across her lower lip. "Very good girl."

He stands abruptly, straightening his jacket. "I'll see you tonight," he states, his eyes flickering between Liv and me. "Both of you."

With a final look, Jax exits the cell, the electronic lock engaging with a definitive click behind him.

The moment he's gone, I round on Olivia. "What the hell was that? Have you completely lost your mind?"

"It's our way out, Aurora," Liv says in a low, urgent

voice. "Don't you see? I need to use his obsession with me to blindside him."

"By what? Sleeping with him?" I hiss, incredulous.

"By making him trust me enough to let his guard down," she counters. "He's careful around you because he knows you hate him, but he thinks he's breaking me. I can use that."

I shake my head, trying to process this. "How exactly will we escape when we're drugged every night? Did you forget that part of his sick little game?"

Liv's eyes dart to the water bottle Jax forced her to drink, then to the steel toilet in the corner of our cell. Her expression shifts from despair to determination.

"I know how to fix this," she whispers. She staggers toward the toilet, dropping to her knees beside it.

"What are you—" I begin, but before I can finish, Liv sticks her fingers down her throat. She retches violently, her body convulsing as she empties the contents of her stomach into the toilet.

She wipes her mouth with the back of her hand and nods toward me. "Your turn now."

I stare at her, not immediately understanding.

"The water, Aurora. Get it out of your system." Her voice is raw but urgent. "If we're not drugged, we can stay awake. And when he comes back tonight..."

The realization hits me. "Genius," I breathe. If Jax thinks we're unconscious, but we're awake and alert...

I rush to the toilet as Liv moves aside, and I push my finger down my throat, gagging immediately. It takes several attempts before my body finally responds, expelling the water I'd consumed earlier—earlier than Liv.

The acidic taste in my mouth is disgusting, but the

clarity in my mind is worth it. I spit repeatedly, trying to clear the bitter taste.

"Do you think it worked?" I ask, wiping my streaming eyes. "What if it's already in our bloodstream?"

"I don't know," Liv admits. "But it's better than doing nothing. We have to try."

I glance at the security camera mounted in the corner of our cell. "He'll have seen us throw up."

Liv shakes her head. "I doubt it, as he only just left. We need to act drugged when he comes. Make him think his plan worked."

I flush the toilet and slump back against the wall, my throat raw and my mouth still tasting of bile. Despite the discomfort, my mind feels sharper than it has in days. I look at Liv, who's already settled back on her cot, arranging herself in a position that mimics drugged sleep.

"We need to practice," she whispers, eyes closed but body tense. "Slow breathing. Completely limp. Not even a twitch when he..." She doesn't finish the sentence, but I understand.

My heart hammers against my ribs as I consider what's ahead.

"What if it doesn't work?" I whisper, moving to my own cot. "What if there's still enough of the drug in our system?"

Liv opens one eye. "Then we try again tomorrow. And the next day."

I practice relaxing my muscles one by one, forcing my breathing to become deep and even. It's surprisingly difficult to appear genuinely unconscious—my body wants to tense, to prepare for fight or flight.

"We'll only get one shot at this," I murmur. "If he realizes we're awake..."

"He won't," Liv says with quiet determination. "Men like Jax are so confident in their power, they don't imagine anyone could outsmart them."

I think of Hunter, wondering if he would say the same about me. The thought sends a pang through my chest. Is he still searching? Has he given up?

"When he comes in," Liv continues, "we wait until he's... distracted. Then we strike. Together."

The plan is terrifying and brilliant in its simplicity. No complex escape scheme, just two desperate women with the element of surprise on their side. If we can overpower Jax, we might be able to use his access to escape.

"It might actually work," I breathe, a tiny spark of hope flickering to life within me.

For the first time since our capture, I feel something beyond despair—a dangerous, fragile optimism. It's mixed with gut-wrenching fear, but it's there.

11

HUNTER

My reflection in the window looks like a stranger's—hollow eyes, three-day stubble, and a jawline tight enough to crack. Blood stains my shirt cuffs. I don't remember if it's mine or someone else's anymore.

"Negative on the western quadrant." Blaze's voice crackles through the comms. "Place is cleared."

I slam my fist into the dashboard. Four more fucking locations. Four more dead ends. Each one meticulously staged to keep us hunting, to keep me suffering.

"Hunter, we need to regroup," Penn says from the driver's seat, glancing at me with poorly concealed concern. "You haven't slept in—"

"I'll sleep when Aurora's safe," I cut him off, pulling up the satellite image of our next target on my tablet. The screen blurs before my eyes, and I blink hard to focus. "The warehouse in Brighton is next. Ten minutes out. Have the team ready."

Penn doesn't start the engine. "We've hit seven locations in three days. Our men are exhausted. You're exhausted."

"I don't care."

"You should." Blaze's voice comes from behind as he approaches our vehicle. He opens the rear door and slides in. "You're making mistakes. That last raid—you went in without proper recon. Two of our men took bullets."

"They'll live," I mutter.

"This time." Blaze's tone hardens. "Next time they might not. And neither might you."

I turn to face him, rage boiling through my veins. "You think I give a fuck about my safety right now? Jax has Aurora. Every minute we waste, he—"

"That's exactly what he wants," Penn interrupts. "You're playing his game, walking into every trap he sets because you're not thinking straight. You're just reacting."

I know they're right. Somewhere in the rational corner of my mind that hasn't been consumed by desperation, I recognize the truth in their words. But that part grows smaller by the hour.

"We need a new approach," Blaze says quietly. "Intelligence over brute force. Jax is feeding us breadcrumbs, and we're following them exactly as he planned."

The tablet in my hand suddenly seems too heavy. My vision swims with exhaustion and something else—fear. Pure, unfiltered fear that I'll never find her. That I've failed her.

"Six hours," Penn says. "Give yourself six hours of sleep. Let us work the intelligence angle. We'll wake you the moment we have something solid."

"I'll rest when we're done with Brighton," I tell them, my voice leaving no room for argument. "Now drive."

Penn exchanges a look with Blaze before reluctantly

starting the engine. The tension in the car is thick enough to cut, but I don't care. Every minute wasted is another minute Aurora remains in Jax's hands.

Forty minutes later, we're approaching a dilapidated warehouse in the industrial district. Rain pelts the windshield as we pull up two blocks away. Our team assembles silently, checking weapons and comms.

"East and west entrances covered," Grayson reports. "Thermal shows seven heat signatures inside the main floor."

I check my weapon and move toward the front, ignoring the concerned glances from my team. My hands shake slightly—from exhaustion or adrenaline, I can't tell anymore.

"Hunter, we need to coordinate—" Ari starts.

"Follow my lead," I cut him off, already moving.

The warehouse door gives way under my boot. I charge through the entrance, weapon raised, scanning for targets. Everything narrows to tunnel vision—finding Aurora is all that matters.

A flash of movement to my right. I pivot, firing two rounds before fully registering what I'm seeing. Return fire erupts from behind a stack of crates.

"Hunter, get down!" Ari shouts.

I ignore him, advancing when I should be taking cover. Something feels off about this place—it's another setup, another of Jax's games—but the rage propels me forward.

The distinctive red dot of a laser sight appears on my chest.

I freeze, a split-second of clarity cutting through my fog of exhaustion.

Suddenly, Ari slams into me from behind, shoving me

sideways as a shot cracks through the air. We crash to the ground behind a concrete pillar. Ari grunts in pain.

"Fuck," he hisses, clutching his shoulder. Blood seeps between his fingers.

"Man down!" Blaze calls over comms. "East section, need immediate cover!"

I stare at the spreading crimson on Ari's shirt. He took a bullet meant for me because I couldn't wait. Because I couldn't think.

The realization hits me with devastating clarity: I'm out of control, and my recklessness just got one of my oldest friends shot.

I STUMBLE into my penthouse at 3 AM, drenched in rain and defeat. The silence crushes me. For days, I've been running on rage, pushing away anything that threatens my focus.

But here, alone, with no one watching, something breaks.

My hands tremble as I pour a whiskey and miss the glass entirely. The amber liquid pools on the counter, and suddenly I can't breathe. Can't think. Can't function.

"FUCK!" I hurl the empty glass against the wall, watching it shatter into a thousand glittering pieces. The sound isn't satisfying enough.

I move to my office in a trance, seeing Aurora's face in every shadow. The weight I've been holding at bay crashes down all at once—crushing, suffocating, unbearable. I sweep everything from my desk in one violent motion. My monitor crashes to the floor. Papers flutter like dying birds.

Not enough.

I overturn the heavy mahogany desk with a roar that

tears my throat. My carefully ordered world splinters apart as I destroy everything within reach. A framed photo of the Vipers shatters under my boot. The glass cabinet housing rare whiskeys explodes under the force of a chair thrown at full strength.

With each act of destruction, my mind grows clearer. My breaths come easier. The fog of exhaustion recedes just enough for rational thought to penetrate.

Fifteen minutes later, my office lies in ruins around me, and I stand in the center, bleeding from cuts I don't remember receiving. The rage has burned itself out, leaving cold clarity in its wake.

Aurora needs me functioning. Not this broken shell staggering through days without sleep.

I make my way to the bedroom, not bothering to clean the blood from my hands. My body feels weighed with lead as I collapse onto the sheets fully dressed. Sleep has been my enemy, bringing nightmares of what might be happening to Aurora. But now I know it's my only ally.

I shut my eyes, forcing my racing mind to quiet. Six hours. I'll allow myself six hours of unconsciousness. Then I'll find her.

For her, I'll rest. For her, I'll think clearly again.

12

AURORA

I lie motionless on the hard cot, my body heavy and my mind foggy. The drugs Jax forced on us aren't fully out of our systems—I feel drunk, disoriented, but not unconscious as he intended. Our plan worked, at least partially. We managed to vomit most of the drugged water, though not quickly enough to escape its effects entirely, particularly me, since I drank it before Liv.

Across the cell, Liv's chest rises and falls in a convincing imitation of deep sleep. We've been rehearsing this moment for hours, whispering back and forth until we heard footsteps approaching.

The electronic lock disengages with a soft click. My heart hammers against my ribs, but I keep my breathing even, my eyes nearly closed—open just enough to see through my lashes.

Jax enters. Even in my peripheral vision, his presence dominates the room. He moves with predatory confidence toward Liv's cot. My stomach twists with dread and hatred.

"Beautiful," he murmurs, reaching down to brush a strand of hair from her face.

I watch through squinted eyes as he sits beside her, the mattress dipping under his weight. Liv remains perfectly still. We'd agreed—she'll wait until he's distracted, until his guard is down. One clean punch to the throat or groin, then we both attack.

Jax turns Liv onto her back with surprising gentleness. His hands slide down to the hem of her nightgown, pushing the fabric up her thighs. The sight makes me sick, but I force myself to remain still. Just a few more seconds...

Liv's eyes flash open. Her fist swings upward toward his face with all her strength.

But Jax catches her wrist mid-air, his reflexes impossibly fast.

"Did you really think I wouldn't notice?" His laugh is cold. "You stupid girls. I watched you vomit the drugs through the cameras."

Liv struggles beneath him, but he pins both her wrists with one hand.

I launch myself from my cot, abandoning all pretense. "Get off her!"

I make it three steps before strong arms wrap around me from behind. I hadn't even noticed the guard entering behind Jax. He lifts me off my feet as I kick and scream, restraining me effortlessly while Jax turns his attention back to my sister.

Jax grips Liv's chin, forcing her to look at him. "You know what I find amusing?" His voice drops to a dangerous whisper. "How you pretend to your sister that you're only responding to me because you're trying to manipulate the situation." His eyes flick toward me, making sure I'm watching. "But we both know the truth, don't we?"

Liv twists her face away. "Go to hell."

"Your body betrays you, sweetheart." His hand slides between her legs, making her flinch. "I've never felt a cunt get so wet just from touching my cock. You can lie to Aurora all you want about your little *plan*, but your body doesn't lie."

I thrash against the guard's grip. "Stop it! Leave her alone!"

Jax ignores me completely. He shoves Liv's dress up higher, exposing her. "Let me show your sister exactly how much you don't want this."

"Don't look, Aurora," Liv cries out, her voice breaking. "Please don't look."

I squeeze my eyes shut as Jax positions himself between my sister's legs. The guard holding me forces my head up, but I keep my eyes downcast, staring at the concrete floor.

The sounds are unbearable—Liv's strangled gasps, Jax's deliberate, wet noises. My stomach heaves. I feel as though I'm dissolving from the inside out, my bones turning to water. The helplessness is crushing me.

"Look at your sister, Aurora," Jax commands.

I keep my eyes fixed on the floor.

"I said LOOK!"

I shake my head, tears streaming down my face. The nausea is overwhelming. My sister is being violated feet away from me, and I can do nothing. Nothing.

The guard's fingers dig into my scalp, wrenching my head upward. I try to keep my eyes closed, but he twists my hair so sharply that pain forces them open.

"Watch," Jax commands from between my sister's legs, his voice thick with satisfaction. "Watch how much she loves it."

I try to look away, but the guard holds me immobile. My

vision blurs with tears as Jax buries his face between Liv's thighs. His hands grip her hips, holding her in place as his tongue works against her.

The most confusing part is Liv's response. Her back arches off the cot, her fingers clutching at the thin mattress. A moan escapes her lips—not pained, not frightened, but something else entirely.

"Jax," she gasps.

This can't be happening. It must be the drugs. She's faking it. She must be faking it.

But her body responds to him with unmistakable pleasure. Her hips move against his mouth, seeking more contact. Her cheeks flush pink. Her breathing quickens.

"Tell your sister how good it feels," Jax demands, lifting his head momentarily.

"So good," Liv moans, sounding drugged, distant. But we vomited most of it out. This can't be from the drugs alone.

Jax returns his mouth to her, and Liv cries out. Her entire body tenses, then trembles. She calls his name again, louder this time, as her body convulses. Clear fluid gushes from between her legs, soaking the mattress beneath her.

"See that?" Jax turns to me, his mouth glistening. "Your sister squirts when she comes." He looks back at Liv. "Did Ari ever make you do that?"

My sister—who I thought was pretending, who said she was playing along to find an escape—is lying there panting, her eyes unfocused, her body still shuddering with aftershocks.

The confusion on my face must be exactly what Jax wanted to see. He smiles, brushing Liv's hair back almost tenderly.

"Your sister's been keeping secrets," he says.

Jax rises to his knees on the cot, towering over my sister's spent body. His hands move to his belt, the metallic clink echoing in our concrete prison. I try to close my eyes, but the guard yanks my hair again, forcing my gaze forward.

"You're going to watch every second of this," Jax says, his voice thick with arousal.

He unzips his pants and pulls out his erection, hard, flushed, and huge. I want to vomit, to scream, to disappear into the floor—anything but witness this. But the guard's grip is unrelenting.

Jax positions himself between Olivia's spread legs but doesn't enter her. Instead, he takes his cock in hand and begins rubbing it against her exposed flesh, sliding it up and down her wetness.

"Look how wet you've made me," he says to Olivia, looking down at where clear fluid leaks from the tip of him onto her body. "I'm not going to fuck you yet, though. Not until you beg for it." He continues the slow, teasing motion, coating himself in her arousal, mixing it with his own. "But I would love to come all over this pretty pussy. Make even more of a mess of you."

I feel tears streaming down my face. This nightmare seems endless, stretching into some eternal hell where I'm forced to watch my sister's violation without being able to stop it.

Liv moans beneath him, her hips lifting slightly off the cot toward his cock. Her face is turned away from me, her eyes fixed solely on Jax as if I don't exist, as if she's forgotten I'm even in the room. The sound of her pleasure cuts through me like a knife.

"That's it," Jax murmurs to her. "Show your sister how much you want it."

"Fuck, yes!" Liv moans, her body arching toward Jax's. The sound of my sister's pleasure pierces my heart like shattered glass.

Jax increases his pace, grinding himself against her center. His cock slides against her clit with deliberate pressure, not entering her but creating friction that makes her gasp and writhe beneath him.

"You love this, don't you?" Jax growls, his voice thick with arousal. "Look at you, spreading your legs for the man who kidnapped you." He grips her thigh harder, leaving fingerprint bruises on her pale skin. "Such a dirty little slut. What would Ari think if he could see you now?"

Liv's head thrashes from side to side, her blonde hair spilling across the thin mattress. She still won't look at me, won't acknowledge my presence as she surrenders to him.

"Tell me who you belong to," Jax demands, rutting against her faster. "Say it!"

"You," she gasps, tears leaking from the corners of her eyes even as her hips lift to meet his. "I belong to you, Jax."

His movements become erratic, his breathing harsh. "I'm going to mark you," he snarls. "Going to come all over this pretty cunt while your sister watches. Show her what happens to girls who play games with me."

Liv's moans grow higher, more desperate. "Please," she begs, "don't stop—fuck—yes!"

Her second orgasm hits her with visible force. Her entire body convulses beneath him as she cries out his name.

Jax grips himself with one hand, still rubbing against her with the head of his cock as he reaches his own climax. White liquid spurts onto my sister's exposed flesh, marking her as he promised.

The guard's grip suddenly loosens. He shoves me away with such force that I stumble across the concrete floor, barely catching myself before colliding with the wall.

I scramble to my cot, curling into the tightest ball possible. My back faces the room, faces them. I pull my knees to my chest, wrapping my arms around them, trying to make myself as small as I can. If I could disappear completely, I would.

The sound of rustling clothes and shifting weight fills the silence. I squeeze my eyes shut, but I can't block out the noises—wet, soft sounds of kissing, my sister's breathless little moans. The mattress creaks as they move together.

"Perfect," Jax murmurs, his voice thick with satisfaction. "You're absolutely perfect, my little slut."

Olivia whimpers something in response that I can't make out.

"Shh," he soothes. "We'll continue this tomorrow. I have plans for you."

The electronic lock disengages again. Footsteps cross the concrete floor—Jax's heavy tread and the guard's boots behind him. The door opens, then closes with a final-sounding clang.

Silence descends. I can hear Liv's ragged breathing from across the room, but I don't turn around. I can't. How could she respond to him like that? Was it all an act? It couldn't have been. No one's that good an actress.

The cot across from mine squeaks. Fabric rustles as she adjusts her clothing.

"Aurora," she whispers.

I curl tighter into myself, pressing my forehead against my knees. I can't talk to her right now. Can't face her. Can't process what I've just witnessed.

"Aurora, please," she tries again.

I remain frozen, every muscle locked in place. The shock is too raw, the shame of not being able to stop Jax too overwhelming.

The silence stretches between us, thick with unspoken words.

13

HUNTER

Something yanks me from oblivion—a persistent, shrill sound cutting through darkness. My eyes snap open, disoriented, mind struggling to place myself.

My phone. It's my fucking phone.

I grab it from the nightstand, squinting at the screen. 6:17 PM. Jesus Christ. I've been out for over six hours.

"What?" I bark into the phone, rage bubbling through me. Six goddamn hours wasted while Aurora is still out there.

"Hunter." It's Ari's voice, tense but controlled. "I think we found them."

Those words hit me like a shot of adrenaline straight to the heart. I'm already on my feet, moving.

"Where?" I demand, glancing down to see I'm still fully dressed—jeans, black T-shirt, boots. I slept in my fucking clothes.

"The old Blackwell psychiatric facility," Ari says. "The one that shut down three years ago. Grayson intercepted communications between two of Jax's lieutenants. They mentioned transferring *the package* to the east wing's secure area."

I grab my gun from the bedside table, checking the magazine. "How solid is this intel?"

"It's the first real lead we've had. The timing of activity there matches up with their disappearance, and Blaze confirmed unusual power consumption at the facility over the past week."

"I'm on my way. Have everyone ready to move in thirty." I'm already striding toward the door, grabbing my jacket. "And Ari—if this is another fucking dead end—"

"It's not," he cuts me off. "Penn's drone picked up heat signatures in the lower level. Multiple bodies, consistent with guard rotations."

My hand tightens around the phone. "I'll be right there."

I end the call, shoving the phone in my pocket as I head for the elevator.

This time, I'm coming for her. And I'm burning everything in my path.

The tension in my penthouse is electric as we gather around the holographic display. Grayson manipulates the 3D rendering of the Blackwell psychiatric facility, highlighting security positions in red.

"Three guard rotations, eight-hour shifts," he explains, zooming in on the perimeter. "External cameras cover every approach with minimal blind spots. Motion sensors throughout the grounds."

"What about access points?" I ask as I study the building's layout. My patience is razor-thin after days of false leads.

Blaze points to a maintenance tunnel. "Underground service entrance here. It's monitored, but their power grid has a vulnerability. We can create a three-minute window by triggering a surge in the north sector."

Penn circles the table, tapping his combat knife against his palm. "Those three minutes won't be enough to extract two hostages through hostile territory."

"It's enough to get us inside," I counter. "Once we're in, we split into two teams. Penn and I take the east wing, where the secure area is located. Ari, Blaze, and Grayson handle perimeter security and provide extraction."

The elevator chimes unexpectedly. All five of us draw weapons simultaneously, aiming at the doors.

When they slide open, Derek Harrison stands there, flanked by two of his security personnel. His eyes lock with mine, cold with fury.

"Reed," he says, voice dangerously calm as he steps forward, ignoring our weapons. "I believe you have something to tell me about my daughters."

I signal the others to stand down. "This isn't a good time, Derek."

"My daughters have been missing for a week," he snarls, advancing toward me. "And suddenly I find you planning what looks like a military operation rather than working with authorities."

I holster my weapon, meeting his gaze. "The authorities can't help with this."

"What have you done?" Derek demands, grabbing my shirt. His security tenses but doesn't move. "Where are they?"

"Jax King has them," I state flatly.

Derek's face goes pale. He knows the name—of course he does. In our circles, everyone knows Jax.

I watch the color drain from Derek's face as Jax's name lands between us. His grip on my shirt loosens.

"Jax King," he repeats. "Why would he—"

"Because of me." I cut him off. No point in lying now. "He took them to get to me."

Derek's security guys exchange glances. One reaches for his weapon.

"I wouldn't," Penn says casually from behind me, the click of his safety releasing unmistakable.

"Stand down," Derek commands his men without looking at them. His eyes remain fixed on mine, processing what I've just revealed. "And you expect me to believe you're going to rescue them? After you put them in danger in the first place?"

"Yes," I say simply. "And you're going to help us."

Derek's laugh is harsh. "Why the hell would I do that?"

"Because we have what you don't," I gesture to the tactical display. "Intel on where they are, a team ready to move, and experience dealing with Jax."

"I can call in—"

"Nothing," I interrupt. "You call in anyone, and Jax will know. He has people everywhere. That's why we're handling this ourselves."

Grayson steps forward. "Mr. Harrison, with respect, we've been working this situation for seven days. We have a narrow window to extract your daughters. Any delay jeopardizes that opportunity."

Derek looks between us, calculation replacing shock in his eyes. "What do you need from me?"

I nod to Blaze, who brings up building schematics. "The facility's main electrical systems. Access codes to bypass Harrison Industries' security protocols that were installed when your company briefly considered purchasing the property."

"You knew about that?" Derek asks, surprised.

"I know everything about you, Derek," I say coldly. "Now, are you going to help get your daughters back, or waste more of our time?"

Derek's jaw tightens as he weighs his options, hatred for me evident in every tense line of his face.

"Fine," he says finally. "I'll make the calls. My connections at the Department of Defense can create a training exercise zone around the perimeter. It'll restrict air traffic and civilian access." His eyes narrow. "But if anything happens to my daughters—"

"Save the threats," I cut him off. "We both know what's at stake."

He leaves to make calls while I turn back to my team.

"We move in ninety minutes," I announce.

Grayson uploads the building schematics Derek provided to our tactical displays. "Power grid override codes are working. We'll have full control of their systems."

"Once we're inside," I continue, "we maintain strict radio discipline. Jax will have signal jammers, so we'll use mesh network comms. If you get separated, regroup at the extraction point."

Penn approaches, voice lowered. "You know Jax won't let them go without a fight. His reputation—"

"I don't give a fuck about his reputation," I growl, sliding a serrated blade into my boot sheath. "Anyone standing between Aurora and me dies. Simple as that."

Ari, arm in a sling from taking a bullet meant for me, looks grimly determined as he checks his gear one-handed. Blaze distributes specialized ammunition—hollow points modified for maximum tissue damage.

"This isn't just a rescue," I tell them, my voice ice cold as I address the room. "This is war. Jax made his choice when he took what's mine."

I slide the final magazine into place with a satisfying click.

"No prisoners. No mercy. We're not coming back until they're safe and Jax is dead."

The van reeks of gun oil and adrenaline as we pull away from my building. Derek's connections bought us a clear path—traffic diverted, police patrols redirected. Every second matters now.

I check my watch: 20:47. Thirteen minutes until the power surge creates our window.

"Timeline?" I demand.

"Satellite shows minimal external movement," Blaze replies, eyes on his tablet. "Heat signatures still present in the lower level."

My jaw clenches so hard I taste blood. Seven days. Seven fucking days she's been in Jax's hands. Seven days I've failed her.

The van hits a pothole, and weapons clatter against metal. No one speaks. They know better. The rage building inside me has nowhere to go but forward—into Jax's men, into anyone standing between Aurora and me.

"Two minutes," Penn announces as we approach the facility's perimeter.

The abandoned psychiatric hospital looms ahead, a grotesque monument to suffering. I imagine Aurora in one of those cells, terrified, waiting, wondering if I'll find her.

I will find her. I fucking will.

"Now," Grayson says, triggering the power surge.

We move in perfect synchronization, breaching the maintenance tunnel entrance exactly as planned. The facility's lower levels smell of mildew and disinfectant as we methodically clear corridors, eliminating three guards who never get the chance to radio for help.

We reach the secure area in the east wing. The door is partially open.

Wrong. Something's wrong.

I signal the others to cover me as I move forward, gun raised. The room beyond is empty—clinical, sterile, recently occupied. A discarded water bottle, still wet. A blanket on the floor.

"Hunter," Penn calls from the adjoining room. "You need to see this."

On the wall, written in what looks like lipstick.

BETTER LUCK NEXT TIME, HUNTER.

My fist slams into the concrete wall. Blood sprays from my knuckles, but I feel nothing except the hollowness of failure and white-hot rage. We missed them by minutes. Fucking minutes.

"I'll kill him," I whisper, voice breaking. "I swear to god, I'll tear him apart."

The words on the wall blur as red washes over my vision. Jax is toying with me. Making this personal. A game where Aurora is the prize and I'm always one step behind.

14

AURORA

I've lost track of time in this concrete hell.

The cell door slides open. I don't even bother looking up anymore.

"Good morning, Aurora." Jax's voice carries that same smugness it always does. "I thought we might have a chat today. Just you and me."

I stay curled on my cot, refusing to acknowledge him.

"I brought something I think you'll find interesting." The scrape of a chair across concrete. "About your father."

My head snaps up involuntarily.

Jax grins. "Finally got your attention." He holds up a tablet. "Did you know there were security cameras at your father's cliff house? The footage was archived in our system."

"What are you talking about?"

"Your daddy's suicide." He spits the last word. "That's what everyone believes happened, right? Poor little Aurora's father jumped off a cliff."

My throat tightens. "Don't."

Jax turns the tablet toward me. "But what if I told you that it wasn't suicide at all?"

The screen shows grainy security footage. Date stamp: twelve years ago. I recognize the cliff edge behind my father's house.

My father stands at the precipice, his back to the camera. Another figure approaches—younger, but I'm sure it's Jax.

"No," I whisper.

They appear to argue. Then Jax lunges forward, shoving my father hard. My father's arms windmill as he tries to catch his balance, but he falls backward.

Out of sight. Off the cliff.

Jax turns to the camera and smiles.

And then I see men running toward him, and it cuts off.

I can't breathe. My entire body trembles as twelve years of grief transform into something darker, more volatile.

"It was him or me," Jax says, casual as if discussing the weather. "My initiation into the Vipers."

Tears stream down my face as I stare at the frozen image of Jax's triumphant smile.

"You murdered him," I whisper.

"I liberated him," Jax corrects. "And now you understand what kind of man you're dealing with."

The footage plays again. This time with sound.

"Please, Jax. I have a family. Daughter." My father's voice—God, his voice—something I'd started to forget. "We can work together in the Vipers. There's room for both—"

"There's only room for one of us," Jax cuts him off. "And I beat you to the punch."

My father stumbles backward as Jax advances. "My daughter—"

"Should've thought about them before trying to join our ranks." Jax's face remains expressionless as he closes the distance. "The position is mine now."

"Don't do this—"

The rest happens in sickening slow motion. My father struggles against Jax's grip, his desperate pleas filling the room. Then the final push. The moment of suspension. The horrifying disappearance from frame.

All while Jax watches, his face a mask of cold indifference—the exact same expression he's wearing now as he observes my breakdown.

Twelve years of guilt crash down around me. The therapy. The anger. The question that haunted me since that day: why did he leave us? The way Mom withered away, drowning her grief until she met Derek.

All of it built on a lie.

"You destroyed my family." My voice sounds foreign, distant. "My mother died believing he killed himself. I spent my entire life wondering why he would abandon us."

"Collateral damage." Jax shrugs. "Your father wanted into the Vipers. I needed the position more. Business is business."

I think of the cliff edge where I stood that day Hunter found me. How I'd been trying to understand what would drive my father to jump. The guilt I carried, thinking I should have seen the signs, should have somehow saved him.

"I believed he jumped." The words scrape my throat. "I was so angry with him—" I choke on a sob. "I thought he chose to leave us."

"And now you know." Jax closes the video. "He didn't."

Something inside me shatters. The careful walls I've built around my grief for twelve years dissolve into white-hot rage. My vision narrows to Jax's smirking face—the face of the man who murdered my father, who destroyed my family, who's been tormenting my sister.

I launch myself at him without thinking. My nails rake across his cheek, drawing blood before he can react. I'm screaming—raw, animal sounds I didn't know I could make. My fists pound against his chest, his face, anywhere I can reach.

"You killed him! You murdered my father!"

Jax's momentary surprise fades quickly. He catches my wrists in one fluid motion, his strength making my furious struggle meaningless. I kick at him, connecting with his shin, but he barely flinches.

"There she is," he says, almost admiringly. "That fire I've heard so much about."

I spit in his face. The glob lands on his cheek, mixing with the blood from my scratches. His expression darkens for just a moment before returning to that calculated calm.

In one swift movement, he spins me around, pulling my back against his chest. His arm wraps around my throat—not choking, just restraining. I writhe against him, but it's like fighting against steel cables.

"Careful now," he murmurs into my ear. "We wouldn't want to waste all that beautiful rage."

I'm still struggling, tears streaming down my face, when he delivers the final blow.

His lips brush my ear as he whispers, "Hunter knew. He's known ever since. He was there. And he never told you."

My body goes limp in his grip. The words hit harder than any physical blow could.

"What?" My voice is barely audible.

"Your precious Hunter." Jax's voice is gentle now,

almost kind. "He was there that day. A new Viper recruit who was watching his first execution. He's known all along what really happened to Daddy."

I go still in Jax's grip, his words sucking all the fight from my body. Hunter knew. Hunter was there. Hunter watched my father die.

"That's not true." The words come out hollow, automatic.

Jax releases me, confident I'm no longer a threat. I stagger forward, falling to my knees on the concrete.

"It is true." His voice carries a false sympathy that makes my stomach turn. "Your lover boy was being initiated that day, too. Watched the whole thing. Never said a word to you, did he?"

The room spins around me. I press my palms against the cold floor, trying to ground myself, but I'm falling, drowning, disappearing into a void where nothing makes sense anymore.

Hunter's face appears in my mind. His intensity when he pulled me from that same cliff edge. The way he looked at me that first time. All this time, he knew.

Every touch. Every kiss. Every whispered promise.

Something inside me goes quiet. The rage, the grief, the betrayal—they're still there, but distant now, like they belong to someone else. I feel myself retreating deeper inside to a dark, cold place where nothing can touch me.

I rise to my feet, my movements mechanical. When I meet Jax's eyes, I see a flicker of uncertainty. He expected tears, hysteria, more rage. Not this emptiness.

"Thank you for telling me," I say. "I needed to know the truth."

Jax studies me, his head tilted. "Interesting. Most people break when they learn something like this."

"I'm already broken." The words come from somewhere far away. "You can't break what's already shattered."

I walk back to my cot and sit down with my hands folded in my lap. I feel nothing. Not pain, not fear, not even hate. Just a vast, expanding darkness where my heart used to be.

Jax watches me, fascinated by this transformation. He's waiting for the crack in my composure, the moment when I collapse under the weight of this revelation.

But there's nothing left to collapse. I've become a hollow vessel, filled only with shadows.

15

AURORA

I count the drips. One. Two. Three. Somewhere in this dank cell, water collects and falls, marking time like a broken metronome. Twelve days. I've been held captive for twelve days.

After I attacked Jax, they drugged us both. I remember the needle, the burn as something cold spread through my veins, and then nothing. When I woke up, Olivia was gone.

This new place is different. Colder. The walls sweat, and the air feels heavy in my lungs. Underground, I think. I can hear water—not just the dripping, but something larger. A river, maybe, or the ocean. The sound ebbs and flows, a constant reminder of a world I can no longer reach.

My cell is smaller than before. A metal cot with a thin mattress. A bucket in the corner. No windows. The light comes from a single bulb behind a wire cage, flickering occasionally as if it might give up at any moment.

I haven't seen Jax since he told me about my father. About Hunter. The guards who bring food don't speak, don't look at me. I've become a ghost to them, something less than human.

"Where's my sister?" I asked the first time the slot opened, and a tray appeared. Silence. "Where am I?" Nothing. "What do you want from me?" The slot closed.

Since then, I've stopped asking.

I worry Hunter will never find me now. If Jax had moved us to throw him off, it would have worked. And even if Hunter does find me... would I want him to? The man who watched my father die and never told me.

I wrap my arms around myself, try to generate warmth. My body feels distant, disconnected. I've retreated so far inside myself that physical discomfort barely registers anymore.

The worst part is being separated from Olivia. Whatever happened between her and Jax, whatever complicated mess that was, she's still my sister. And now I don't even know if she's alive.

The door scrapes open. I don't bother looking up until his shadow falls across the floor.

"Aurora." Jax's voice is softer than before. Almost gentle. "I brought you something to eat that isn't prison slop."

He sets a paper bag on the edge of my cot. I ignore it. The smell of real food makes my stomach clench, but I won't give him the satisfaction.

"Where's my sister?" I ask, finally meeting his eyes.

His face changes, softens. "Somewhere safe. Somewhere... better than this."

"If you've hurt her—"

"Hurt her?" He laughs, pulling up the metal chair across from my cot. "Olivia is extraordinary. I wouldn't damage something so... precious."

The way he says her name makes my skin crawl.

"You know," he continues, leaning forward, elbows on

his knees, "your father was a lot like Hunter. Brilliant, ambitious."

"You pushed him off that cliff."

"I protected my position in the Vipers." His eyes go distant, reminiscing. "The Vipers needed leadership, direction. Your father wanted to join and lead." He shakes his head. "I wanted to lead."

"So, you murdered him."

"I eliminated a threat. Just like I'm doing with Hunter." He stands, paces the small room. "Men like them don't understand what it takes to create something that lasts."

"You're insane."

"I'm pragmatic. I've spent years protecting the Vipers." His voice rises with conviction. "Every decision, every sacrifice—even this—it's all necessary."

"You're not a hero, Jax. You're a monster."

He smiles, genuinely amused. "We're all monsters, Aurora. Some of us just admit it." His expression shifts again. "Your sister understands. Olivia sees the truth in me. The power."

My hands clench into fists. "If you touch her again, I swear I'll kill you myself."

"Olivia comes to me willingly. She's... magnificent in her surrender."

I lunge at him. "You better not hurt her, or I promise you'll never see it coming."

Jax just smiles. "So much like your father. So naive."

I stare at Jax as he continues his twisted monologue, and clarity washes over me like ice water. This isn't just paranoia—it's complete delusion. His eyes shine with messianic fervor. He genuinely believes he's the hero of this story.

"The Vipers needed protection," he continues, voice

rising with conviction. "Every move I've made—eliminating threats, securing our position—it's all been for the greater good."

In his mind, he's rewritten the murder of my father into an act of noble defense. Pushed a man off a cliff and called it salvation. The realization makes my blood run cold.

"You're not protecting anything," I say flatly. "You're afraid someone might take your power."

His expression hardens. "You don't understand what I've built."

"I understand perfectly. You're a killer who can't stand competition."

His eyes darken. The gentleness from moments ago evaporates, as if it never existed. "I thought you might be different. More like your sister. More... receptive to the truth."

"The truth?" I laugh. "You wouldn't recognize truth if it pushed you off a cliff."

His jaw tightens. "I've been patient with you, Aurora. Too patient." He pulls something from his pocket—a small tablet. The screen glows blue in the dim cell.

Jax turns the tablet toward me, his expression triumphant. "You think Hunter is so different from me? That he's coming to rescue you? Your white knight?"

The screen shows security footage of the cliff—my father's cliff. The same rocky ledge where Hunter pulled me back that day. My stomach twists with dread.

"What is this?" I whisper.

"Watch."

Two figures appear on the cliff. One is unmistakably Hunter. The other man I don't recognize—middle-aged, wearing an expensive suit.

"This was four years ago," Jax says quietly.

Hunter moves closer to the man, backing him toward the edge. The stranger's hands are up, placating, his mouth moving rapidly. Pleading. Hunter's face is cold, expressionless. Nothing like the man I thought I knew.

"No," I breathe. "He wouldn't—"

But he does.

In one swift motion, Hunter lunges forward and shoves the man. There's no hesitation, no struggle. Just a calculatedly violent push, and the stranger disappears over the edge.

Hunter doesn't even look down. He straightens his jacket and walks away.

I can't breathe. The room spins around me as I stare at the empty cliff edge where a man just died. Where my father died.

"Who was he?" I manage to ask, my voice barely audible.

"Does it matter?" Jax's voice sounds distant through the roaring in my ears. "You see it now, don't you? Hunter is exactly like me. We do what's necessary."

The footage loops, playing again. Hunter and the stranger on the cliff. The argument. The push. The casual walk away. Each time it feels like another blow to my chest.

"He saved me there," I whisper. "He pulled me back."

Jax laughs softly. "Did he? Or did he recognize the perfect opportunity to manipulate you?"

My mind reels, questioning everything. Every touch. Every promise. Every moment I thought was real.

Is it possible that the man I've fallen for is a monster like Jax?

16

HUNTER

The bourbon burns my throat but doesn't touch the hollowness inside me. Fourteen days. Three hundred thirty-six hours since Aurora disappeared.

I study the digital map dominating my office wall, red pins marking Jax's properties we've already hit, blue pins indicating targets remaining. The map's getting crowded with red.

"Hunt." Penn appears in the doorway, face grim. Blood spatters his tailored shirt—not his own. "The Northside warehouse is clear. Six of Jax's men were eliminated. No sign of Aurora or her sister."

I nod, not bothering to look up from the satellite images of our next target. "And the intel?"

"Recovered. Four more locations not on our original list."

Four more places to tear apart. Four more facilities to burn to the ground.

"Martinez and Rogers have declared for Jax," Penn continues. "Publicly."

"Let them." The words taste like ash. The Vipers organization I helped build is consuming itself, tearing itself apart at the seams. Half of our members have aligned with me, a third with Jax. The rest are desperately trying to stay neutral in a war that allows no middle ground.

I haven't slept more than two hours at a stretch since that rogue six hours. The edges of my vision blur, but I force clarity through sheer will. I've become precisely what I need to be: a weapon.

"The body count is rising," Penn says quietly. "Sullivan's people hit one of our safe houses in Chelsea. Grayson retaliated—three of Sullivan's lieutenants won't be reporting for duty anymore."

I look up at last. "Any word from our inside source?"

Penn shakes his head. "Nothing since the psychiatric facility. Jax is getting paranoid, limiting information even to his inner circle."

I check my watch. "The next operation begins in forty minutes. Brief the team."

When Penn leaves, I stand before the wall of surveillance photographs. In each one, Jax smiles, unaware he's being watched. In each one, I imagine putting a bullet through his skull.

The Vipers used to rule this city from the shadows. Now we're tearing it apart in plain sight, spilling blood on streets we once controlled silently. Every hour that passes without finding Aurora, I burn another piece of the empire to ash.

And I don't regret a single flame.

Grayson bursts through the door without knocking, tablet in hand. The circles under his eyes match mine, but there's something different—a spark I haven't seen in days.

"I've got something," he says.

My pulse quickens. "Show me."

He swipes through satellite images on the main screen.

"Coastal warehouse complex, forty miles north. Officially owned by Maritime Solutions LLC—a shell company buried under three layers of corporate bullshit."

"We checked all Jax's known shell companies," I say, already moving toward my weapons case.

"This one wasn't on our radar. The property transfer only happened three days ago." Grayson pulls up energy consumption graphs. "Look at the power draw—consistent with subterranean climate control and high-end security systems."

My eyes narrow on the thermal imaging scans. "Those heat signatures..."

"Multiple bodies. Lower level, approximately twenty feet below ground." Grayson zooms in on surveillance photos. "And here's what sealed it—the security rotation. Six-man teams, three-hour intervals."

"Jax's personal detail," I say.

For the first time in two weeks, I feel something beyond rage and exhaustion. Hope—dangerous, fragile hope.

"Satellite confirms four sniper positions, motion sensors throughout the perimeter. Two vehicle checkpoints." Grayson scrolls through more images. "It's a fortress, but it's not impossible."

I study the layout, already mapping entry points, calculating risks. "How recent is this intel?"

"Thermal imaging is from ninety minutes ago. Security footage was accessed thirty minutes ago."

"Wheels up in five. Full tactical gear. I want everybody loaded and ready." I don't look up from the schematics as I issue orders, memorizing every entrance, exit, and potential chokepoint in the warehouse complex.

"Hunt, satellite confirmation will take another forty

minutes," Grayson says, hesitating by the door. "We should wait for—"

"No." The word cuts through the room. "Every minute we wait is another minute she's in his hands. Move. Now."

No one argues further. They've learned better these past two weeks.

Twenty minutes later, our convoy speeds north along coastal roads. Four black SUVs, twenty of my most loyal men. Armed like we're invading a small country. Which isn't far from the truth.

Penn sits beside me in the lead vehicle, checking his weapons. I catch him watching me in my peripheral vision.

"Say it," I order, eyes fixed on the road ahead.

"You haven't slept in three days," Penn says. "Your decision-making is compromised."

"Irrelevant."

"You're taking increasingly reckless actions. The Williamsburg raid—you went in without backup. The dockside facility—you walked directly into crossfire." Penn loads his magazine with a sharp click. "You're not just willing to die for this, you're actively trying to."

I don't bother denying it. "Your point?"

"My point is, we need you functioning to get her out."

"No," I correct him. "You need me to find her. After that, my survival is optional."

Penn shifts to face me directly. "Hunter—"

"I don't need to survive this." I cut him off, meeting his eyes briefly. Something in my expression makes him flinch. "I just need to get Aurora out. That's the mission. The only mission."

"And if we get there and she's not there? If it's another diversion?"

"Then we burn it down and move to the next location."

My knuckles whiten on the steering wheel. "I'll tear down every building Jax has ever touched until I find her. And when I do find her, I'm going to make him beg for death."

The first hints of dawn bleed across the horizon as we approach the compound. We park the vehicles, and I signal to Penn and Grayson, their teams separating to hit the secondary entry points. Perfect timing—guard rotation in twelve minutes, maximum vulnerability.

"On my mark," I whisper into the comm. My shoulder holster feels heavier than usual, loaded with extra magazines. I won't run out this time. I won't fail her again.

"Three. Two. One. Execute."

We breach through three entry points. The shaped charges blow the reinforced doors with precisely calculated force. Before the debris settles, I'm through the opening, weapon raised.

The first guard doesn't even have time to shout before my bullet finds his throat. The second manages to trigger an alarm before dropping. Red emergency lights bathe the corridor in crimson as sirens wail.

"Brace!" Blaze shouts, his rifle chattering as he provides covering fire.

I move without hesitation, each step, each shot, mechanical in its precision. A guard emerges from a side room—dead before he fully clears the doorway. Two more appear at the end of the hall—three rapid shots, two bodies dropping.

"East wing secure," Penn's voice crackles through comms.

"West wing, heavy resistance," Grayson reports, gunfire punctuating his words.

I advance toward the stairwell leading to the lower levels. A bullet tears through my left shoulder, spinning me half around. White-hot pain flares, then immediately recedes behind the wall of adrenaline and purpose.

"Hunter, you're hit," Blaze says, moving to cover me.

"Irrelevant." I switch my weapon to my right hand, continuing forward without breaking stride. Blood soaks my tactical vest, warm against my skin. It doesn't matter. Nothing matters except finding Aurora.

We push toward the basement access, encountering a barricade of Jax's men. Their desperate fire speaks volumes —we're close. We must be close.

"Covering fire," Blaze calls, unleashing a barrage.

I move during the suppression, flanking their position with cold efficiency. Five men. Five shots. Five bodies.

The stairwell to the lower level appears ahead, heavy security door partially open. Blood trails down my arm, dripping from my fingertips as we push deeper into the compound, following the path of bodies we've left behind.

The basement level is silent—too silent. Bodies of Jax's men litter our path, but there's no sign of prisoners. My wound throbs with each heartbeat, but I barely register the pain as I push forward.

"Clear these rooms," I order, gesturing to Blaze and his team. "Find them."

Electronic locks line a corridor of eight cells. I approach the first, pulse hammering in my ears louder than the alarm still wailing above us. Empty.

Second cell. Empty.

Third. Empty.

With each vacant cell, desperation claws deeper into my chest. What if we're too late? What if this is another of Jax's games?

The fourth and fifth cells hold nothing but darkness. My breathing becomes ragged, not from exertion but from the growing fear that we've failed again. That I've failed her again.

Then I reach the last cell. Through the small, reinforced window, I see her.

Aurora.

She's chained to a metal cot, wrists secured with heavy restraints. Her once-vibrant form looks diminished, cheekbones too sharp under her skin, dark shadows beneath her eyes. But she's breathing. She's alive.

For one perfect moment, everything else falls away—the pain, the exhaustion, the war I've waged across the city. None of it matters because I've found her.

Her eyes meet mine, widening with shock. Recognition flares in those azure depths, followed by something I don't expect—something that turns my blood to ice. Her gaze hardens, lips pulling back in a snarl of pure hatred.

She knows.

I blast the electronic lock with a single shot and kick the door open. "Aurora—"

She moves with unexpected speed, lunging from the cot, being pulled back by the chains. I still go to her, and her body slams into mine, fists pounding against my chest and wounded shoulder, sending shards of pain through my body.

"You knew!" she screams, voice raw. "You knew what he did to my father, and you never told me!"

Her nails rake across my face as she attacks with every ounce of strength her weakened body possesses. I don't defend myself. I don't try to stop her. Each blow is deserved.

"You watched him die," she sobs, still striking me. "You watched, and you said nothing!"

Her fists connect with my wounded shoulder, sending

white-hot pain through my body, but I don't flinch. Don't step back.

"I'm sorry," I say, my voice breaking. "I'm so fucking sorry, Aurora. I'll explain everything, but we need to go. Now."

Blood drips from my shoulder, pooling on the concrete floor. I barely notice it. Her eyes—those beautiful eyes that once looked at me with passion—now burn with hatred. It cuts deeper than any bullet.

"Where's Olivia?" Aurora demands, still hitting me even as tears stream down her face. "Where's my sister?"

My stomach drops. Cold dread spreads through me, washing away the momentary relief of finding Aurora.

"All the other cells are empty. I don't know."

Aurora's voice cracks with fear. "Jax said he had special plans for her and kept us separate. We must find her!"

The compound shudders violently, concrete dust raining from the ceiling. The familiar vibration of explosives ripples through the structure. Jax rigged the building to blow—a final contingency if his facility was compromised.

I don't hesitate. I pull bolt cutters from my tactical vest and snap through Aurora's restraints. The chains fall away with a metallic clatter.

"We'll find Olivia, I swear to you," I promise, lifting Aurora into my arms despite her protests. Her body feels painfully light—too many pounds lost during captivity. "But first, I'm getting you out of here."

She struggles against me, fists pounding weakly against my chest. "Put me down! I'm not leaving without her!"

Another explosion rocks the compound. Larger this time. Closer.

"Hunter!" Penn's voice crackles through my comm. "Get out of there. The fucking place is going to collapse!"

I tighten my grip on Aurora and run toward the exit, each step sending fresh agony through my wounded shoulder.

"I can't leave her," Aurora sobs, her fight weakening as exhaustion overtakes her. "She's my sister. I promised I'd protect her."

I cradle Aurora against my chest as we race through the collapsing structure. The guards have abandoned their posts—rats fleeing a sinking ship. Smart. Because Jax has rigged this place to come down on our heads.

Dust fills my lungs with every breath. My wounded shoulder screams with each movement, but I keep Aurora tucked against me, navigating through falling debris.

The building shudders violently. A support beam crashes down mere feet ahead of us. I pivot, carrying Aurora down another corridor.

"Let me run, we'll be faster!" She shrieks.

I nod and set her down on her feet. "This way," I command, pulling her toward an emergency exit. Despite her hatred for me, despite her fury, Aurora keeps pace. Two weeks of Jax's captivity haven't broken her spirit.

"Move!" I yell as the ceiling begins to give way. We sprint the final stretch, bursting through the exit door just as a thunderous roar signals the building's death throes.

Dawn light greets us for one brilliant moment before the shockwave hits. I don't think—just react. I spin, wrapping my body around Aurora as we're thrown forward. My back takes the brunt of the impact as debris rains down. Something sharp tears through my tactical vest, embedding in my flesh. Another impact knocks the breath from my lungs.

When the dust begins to settle, I pull myself up, hands immediately searching Aurora's body. Blood trickles from a gash on her forehead. Her arms are mottled with bruises, some fresh, others yellowing. She's too thin, too pale, but breathing.

"You're okay," I whisper. "You're going to be okay."

Her eyes find mine, still burning with fury and betrayal, but something else flickers there too—the instinct to survive.

My comm crackles to life as Penn's voice cuts through the haze of pain and relief.

"Hunter, Jax escaped. Spotted him heading north with a woman matching Olivia's description. Three vehicles, full security detail."

Aurora's hand shoots out, gripping my wrist with surprising strength. "Liv," she gasps. Her face crumples. "No. No, we can't leave her with him!"

The devastation in her eyes cuts deeper than my wounds. In two weeks of captivity, she hasn't broken. Now she might shatter.

I pull her toward the extraction vehicle, blood still seeping through my tactical vest. "We won't. I promise you, Aurora, we'll get her back."

Even as the words leave my mouth, the tactical reality sinks in. Jax has orchestrated this perfectly, forcing me to choose between securing Aurora's immediate safety and pursuing Olivia. Aurora needs medical attention. She's dehydrated, malnourished, and traumatized. The rational choice is clear.

But rationality means nothing when she looks at me with those eyes.

"He's going to hurt her," Aurora whispers, her voice cracking. "You don't understand what he's capable of."

"I do understand." I tighten my grip on her arm as she tries to pull away. "Better than anyone."

Penn approaches. "Pursuit vehicles are ready. But Hunter—" He glances meaningfully at Aurora's weakened state, then at my blood-soaked shoulder.

"We need to get her secure first," I say, making the decision I hate but know is right. "Then we hunt him down. Full tactical response."

"You promised!" Aurora fights against my grip with renewed strength. "You promised we wouldn't leave her!"

"And we won't," I say firmly. "But I need you safe first."

The sadistic bastard has won this round. He's split us apart, taking the one person who could force Aurora to question whether she can trust me to rescue those she loves.

Her resistance suddenly falters. The adrenaline that kept her going finally ebbs, and her knees buckle beneath her. I catch her before she hits the ground, lifting her into my arms despite the searing pain in my shoulder.

Aurora collapses into the vehicle, physical and emotional exhaustion finally overwhelming her. I hold her trembling body against mine as Grayson passes me the tablet, which shows our tracking systems.

I watch Jax's heat signature disappear from the screen, her sister—my fiancée on paper—vanishing into the darkness with a madman.

17

AURORA

The mountains rise like sentinels outside the window. Indifferent. Unmoved by human suffering. I press my fingertips against the cool glass, leaving smudges that fade within seconds. Just like truth. Just like trust.

Six hours in this place. Six hours of silence. Medical equipment beeps softly in the background—monitoring my vital signs, my physical recovery. The doctor said something about moderate dehydration, malnutrition, and bruised ribs. Words that floated past me without landing.

I haven't spoken since Hunter carried me from that collapsing warehouse. What is there to say when your entire reality has been obliterated?

My father didn't kill himself. He was murdered. And Hunter knew.

The man who touched me, who claimed me, who made me feel things I'd never felt—he was there when my father died and said nothing.

"You need to eat something." Hunter's voice comes from the doorway. I don't turn. Don't acknowledge him.

The mountain view blurs as tears fill my eyes. I blink them back. No more crying. No more weakness.

Somewhere out there, Liv is with Jax. My sister. The thought hollows me out completely. While I sit in this luxurious prison—because that's what it is, despite the comfortable furniture and state-of-the-art security—Liv remains in the hands of a monster.

I press my forehead against the glass and close my eyes.

A blanket settles around my shoulders. I didn't hear him approach.

"Aurora." Hunter's voice is soft, cautious. "The doctor says you're severely dehydrated. You need to drink."

I remain motionless, eyes fixed on the darkening mountains. In my mind, I'm back at the cliff house, standing where my father stood, feeling what he might have felt in his final moments. Did he know? Did he see it coming? Did he think of me?

I sit by the window, the oversized blanket swallowing me like I'm a child again. Outside, darkness creeps across the mountains, shadows climbing higher with every passing minute. I feel Hunter's presence behind me—hovering, waiting. The silence between us has weight, substance.

My reflection wavers in the glass. Hollow eyes. Tangled hair. A stranger's face. I barely recognize myself anymore.

Hunter shifts his weight, wincing. From the corner of my eye, I catch him adjusting the hasty bandage on his shoulder. The bullet wound he received during my rescue. I should care. I should feel something. Instead, there's emptiness where emotion once lived.

Twelve days in a cell with Jax didn't break me. One video did.

My bladder protests, demanding attention. Basic bodily

functions continue even when your world implodes. How inconsiderate.

I push myself up from the window seat, clutching the blanket around my shoulders like armor. Hunter steps forward, hand outstretched.

"Aurora—"

I walk past him without acknowledgment. His hand falls to his side. Good.

The hallway stretches before me, leading to a bathroom I barely remember using earlier. I move on unsteady legs, my bare feet silent against the hardwood floor. On way back from the bathroom, I hear voices drift from the kitchen. Penn's low murmur catches my attention as I leave the bathroom.

"She's going to break her silence eventually," he says. "When she does, it's going to be brutal."

I freeze, hand on the doorknob.

"I know," Hunter replies, his voice rough with exhaustion. "I deserve whatever's coming."

"It's not about deserving," Penn says. "It's about whether you can handle it. She's stronger than you think."

I slip back to the living room before I can hear Hunter's response. Their voices continue, muffled now by the closed door.

They're talking about me like I'm a bomb about to detonate. Maybe I am.

It happens at sunset.

The mountains outside the window transform into silhouettes against a bleeding sky. Crimson and gold spill across the horizon, painting the room in warm light that feels like a mockery of the cold emptiness inside me.

For hours, I've sat immobile, processing fragments of grief while Hunter maintains his vigil. Sometimes he leaves—phone calls, whispered conversations with Penn, bringing food I won't touch. But he always returns, taking up space in the doorway or sitting silently in the chair across from me.

Waiting. Watching. As if I'm the dangerous one.

The dying sunlight catches on something metal across the room—Hunter's watch.

Something breaks inside me. Not like glass shattering, but like ice giving way beneath unsuspecting feet. A sudden plunge into frigid waters.

I stand in one fluid motion, the blanket falling away from my shoulders. My legs should feel weak after hours of sitting, after days of captivity, but rage fuels my strength. I turn to face Hunter directly.

His expression changes when our eyes meet—surprise, then wariness. He recognizes that something has shifted. The silence between us is about to end.

"Tell me everything," I demand, my voice hoarse from screaming during my captivity, from crying, from twelve days of horror. Each word scrapes against my raw throat. "Every detail about my father's death. Why did you never tell me?"

Hunter straightens, his injured shoulder forgotten. His face—that beautiful face I once traced with reverent fingers—hardens into something unreadable. But his eyes... his eyes give him away. There's fear there. Not of me, but of this moment. Of what happens after truth is spoken aloud.

He takes one step toward me, then stops as I instinctively back away.

"Aurora—" he begins, but I cut him off with a raised hand.

"No excuses. No lies." My voice grows stronger with each word. "Just the truth. All of it."

I wrap my arms around myself, watching Hunter's face as he struggles with whatever truth he's about to reveal.

He stands before me, blood seeping through his haphazardly bandaged shoulder. Exhaustion etches deep lines around his eyes. For a moment, I almost feel sorry for him. Almost.

"Your father..." Hunter begins, his voice rough. He clears his throat and tries again. "Your father participated in the hunt. Like the one that happened the night you and I did."

My breath catches. "What?"

"The Vipers have always conducted these trials. Your father tried to become one of us. It's—it's how we test recruits' abilities and their instincts." Hunter's eyes never leave mine. "Sometimes recruits don't make it out alive."

The room tilts slightly. I steady myself against the windowsill.

"Your father knew the risks when he agreed to participate. He wasn't the first to die during Selection."

"So my father was just... collateral damage?" The words taste bitter on my tongue.

Hunter's jaw tightens. "After I saw how you'd processed it—believing it was suicide—I didn't see the point in telling you differently. You'd found a way to live with it."

Something breaks loose inside me—rage, hot and clarifying.

"You didn't see the point?" My voice rises. "Do you have any idea what it did to me, thinking my father chose to leave us? That he jumped off that cliff because staying alive—staying with me—wasn't worth it?"

Hunter remains silent.

"I've spent twelve years wondering what I could have done differently. What I could have said to make him want to stay." Tears blur my vision, but I refuse to let them fall. "And you knew. You knew he didn't choose to die. He was killed. How could you not understand the difference that would make to me?"

Hunter takes a step toward me. "Aurora—"

"No." I hold up my hand. "It was never your choice to make. You watched my father die, and then you touched me, you held me, and you said nothing. And what about Olivia?" My voice cracks. "Where is she right now? With Jax—the man who killed my father?"

Hunter's face contorts with something resembling guilt. "We're doing everything possible to find her."

"Like you did everything possible to be honest with me?" The words fly from me, sharp as broken glass.

He runs a hand through his hair, wincing as the movement pulls at his injured shoulder. "Aurora, there are things about the Vipers you don't understand. Confidentiality is paramount. We take oaths—"

"Confidentiality?" I laugh, a hollow sound that doesn't belong to me. "My father's murder wasn't some corporate secret. It was my life! My trauma!"

"I was bound by—"

"By what? Your precious code?" I step closer, trembling with rage. "While I poured my heart out about standing at that cliff, trying to understand why my father would leave me—you sat there knowing the truth and said nothing."

Hunter reaches for me, but I step back.

"I thought we had something." My voice drops to a whisper. "But it was built on lies."

"What I feel for you is real." His eyes flash with desperation. "More real than anything I've ever felt."

"But not real enough to tell me the truth."

He falls to his knees suddenly, his imposing frame crumpling before me. "Aurora, please." His voice breaks. "I was wrong. I should have told you everything from the beginning."

In another life, seeing Hunter Reed on his knees might have moved me. Now, I feel nothing but a vast emptiness.

"I don't know if I can forgive you for this." The words come out calm. "Not just keeping it from me—but watching it happen. Standing there while Jax pushed my father to his death."

"I didn't know—" He reaches for my hand. "I was twenty-one. A recruit myself. I didn't know who he was. Not until—"

"But you knew after."

His fingers graze mine, but the touch that once electrified now leaves me cold. The disconnect between us stretches like an uncrossable chasm.

"I'll spend the rest of my life making this right," he whispers.

I look down at him, this powerful man brought low, and feel nothing but exhaustion.

"I need space," I whisper. "I can't process any of this with you here."

Hunter looks up at me, still on his knees. For a moment, I think he might argue or try to convince me of something —his love, his regret, his plans to make everything right. Instead, his expression shifts into resignation.

He rises slowly, wounded shoulder making his movement less fluid than usual. The Hunter Reed I thought I knew would never show weakness like this, but perhaps I never really knew him at all.

"I'll be downstairs if you need anything," he says. "Penn and the others are actively tracking Olivia's location. I promise we'll find her."

Another promise. I stare through him rather than at him.

He hesitates at the doorway, looking back at me one last time. "I'm sorry, Aurora. More than you'll ever know."

The door closes with a soft click. His footsteps fade down the hallway.

I stand frozen, listening to the sudden silence. The mountains outside have disappeared into darkness. No more sunset. Just black emptiness pressing against the window.

My legs give out first.

I slide down the wall, hitting the floor harder than expected. The pain barely registers. The first sob rips through me like a physical force, bending me forward until my forehead touches my knees. I wrap my arms around myself, trying to hold the broken pieces together.

Every tear feels like betrayal. I shouldn't be crying over him. I should be focusing on Olivia.

But the tears come anyway, hot and relentless. For my father. For the truth, I never knew. For twelve years of misplaced anger. For my stepsister in the hands of his killer. For the love I thought was real.

I press my palm against my mouth to muffle the sounds, not wanting Hunter to hear me fall apart. Even now, I can't bear the thought of him seeing this final weakness.

18

HUNTER

Dawn breaks through the windows at the end of the hallway, painting the corridor in soft gold. I haven't moved from outside Aurora's door all night. My body aches from hours on the floor, shoulder wound throbbing beneath fresh bandages. None of it matters.

I understand what true fear feels like. That raw, primal terror of losing someone irreplaceable. I've built my empire, destroyed enemies, yet I'm powerless against the locked door separating me from Aurora.

Hours pass in silence. The security team's footsteps echo periodically down the hall, their gazes averted from my uncharacteristic position. Penn brought coffee at 3 AM, saying nothing about finding me slumped against her door.

The handle turns. I scramble to my knees, ignoring the sharp protest from my injured shoulder. The door swings open, revealing Aurora—eyes swollen, face pale, dark hair tangled around shoulders that somehow still look strong despite everything.

She freezes, clearly not expecting to find me here, much

less on my knees before her. I clasp my hands together like a man in prayer.

"I will spend the rest of my life earning your forgiveness," I say. "Not because I expect it, but because you deserve nothing less than complete honesty from this moment forward."

Aurora tries to walk past me, eyes averted, her body language screaming for distance. Without thinking, I catch her hand gently—not gripping, just a touch, something she could break if she wanted to.

"Ask me anything. Everything. No more secrets. No more lies. I swear it." My voice catches, unfamiliar vulnerability scratching my throat.

She stares down at me—at Hunter Reed on his knees, a man who's never begged for anything in his life, now pleading for a chance. Something shifts in those azure eyes. Not forgiveness. Not yet. But perhaps the possibility of it.

"I need to find my sister," she says, voice hollow from renewed grief. "That's all I care about right now."

I nod, still holding her hand like it's the most precious thing I've ever touched. "I have every resource mobilized. Penn's team tracked their movement to a private airfield. We believe they're heading west."

Her fingers tremble in mine, and I fight the urge to pull her close, to shelter her against me. That's not what she needs from me now.

"You knew." It's not a question. "When I stood at that cliff edge wondering why my father would leave me, you knew the truth."

The accusation lands like a physical blow. "Yes, but in my defense, I didn't know who you were at that point. And unfortunately, more than one man has gone over the cliff during initiation."

"How can you say that with so little emotion? How many families have been broken by your Vipers' initiation?"

"Because I'm a monster," I admit simply. "Because I've spent years burying my conscience so deep, I couldn't find it anymore. Until you."

I exhale slowly, my hands shaking slightly. This is the moment I've dreaded since the day I found her on that same cliff.

"We were the first," I begin, voice low. "Five of us—me, Blaine, Ari, Grayson, and Penn. We were approached by a professor, Jax King, if you can believe it, during our final year at Westlake Academy. We helped him build the Vipers from nothing. Your father... he was part of our first official selection, including the six of us. The rules were we all had to pass initiation as recruits. It was before I purchased the house next door to your father's. Jax's contact rented us the house to conduct our first initiation."

Aurora's face remains stone, but her eyes never leave mine.

"Your father was brilliant. Strategic. Connected. Everything we wanted in our ranks." I swallow hard. "And he'd passed every test—pain tolerance, loyalty verification, psychological breaking points. The Hunt was supposed to be the final challenge."

I drop her hand and stand slowly, shoulder throbbing. "Normally, we release multiple candidates into a controlled area. They'd compete against each other while we hunted them. The strongest candidates would win positions."

"Jax was threatened by my father," she says, voice flat.

I nod. "Your father was exceptional. Jax saw him as a threat to his leadership. They'd clashed during earlier phases—your father questioned Jax's methods, his extremes." I pause. "Jax made the decision to personally hunt your father that night and ensure he died."

I remember the moonlight on the cliffs, the distant sound of waves.

"We were all out participating that night. Jax was nowhere to be seen and he'd disabled his tracker, going off grid. By the time we realized something was wrong..."

The memory sears through me—running through the woods, the shouting, arriving by Jax's side just after he pushed her father off.

"We were too late when we got to the cliff edge. I was too far away when Jax lunged forward." My voice breaks. "One push. That's all it took."

Aurora's eyes fill with tears.

"We couldn't stop it. Couldn't reverse it. Jax became our leader that night, and he made it clear—anyone who spoke about what really happened would join your father at the bottom of those rocks."

I look directly into her eyes. "I was a coward. I told myself it wasn't my responsibility. I buried it so deep I could almost forget—until I saw you standing in that same spot."

I take a breath, steeling myself for what comes next. The complete truth. No more secrets between us.

"After your father died, Jax rewrote the narrative. Suicide was cleaner. No questions, no investigation. He had a team plant the evidence—the depression diagnosis, financial troubles that didn't exist. I watched them fabricate the story of a man who chose to leave his family."

Aurora's tears fall silently now, her body rigid with grief.

"Every year on the anniversary, Jax would toast to your father. Called it a *necessary sacrifice* for the organization to become what it was meant to be. The Hunt then became a frequent fight to the death."

I run my hand through my hair. "When I saw you on that cliff, it was like seeing a ghost. I think it's why I went to check on you, I couldn't bear seeing you fall to your death the same way as him."

"And when our eyes met that day on the cliff," I continue, voice dropping lower, "I felt something I'd never experienced before. A connection that went beyond physical attraction. Beyond logic. Something that hit me in places I didn't know existed."

I see the conflict in Aurora's eyes—wanting to hate me, yet unable to deny what had sparked between us. "How about the man you pushed off the cliff yourself?" she demands.

I freeze, my heart stopping for a fraction too long. "He was a traitor in our ranks."

She glares at me. "And that makes it okay?"

I clench my jaw. "No. I don't pretend to be a good man, Aurora. I think you knew that from the moment we met. I have blood on my hands. I've killed, and I'll kill again. That will never change, but I don't think that's really what you are upset about."

Her expression remains unchanged. "No, it's not."

"It's a weird twist of fate that put us both on that cliff edge that night." I laugh without humor, the sound hollow in my chest. "The universe has a sick sense of humor. For years, I avoided emotional attachments, relationships, and anything that might make me vulnerable. Then I see you—this beautiful, fierce woman standing where your father died—and something in me just... broke open."

My hands clench at my sides. "So, I arranged an engagement with the wrong sister, never once thinking the woman I couldn't get out of my head could be the daughter of the man I watched Jax push off that cliff twelve years ago."

Aurora's face darkens with pain, her body going rigid. The cruel irony hangs between us like a physical thing.

"When I learned who you really were, I ignored it, carried on pursuing what I wanted. The right thing to do would have been to walk away. I should have ended things with Olivia immediately and disappeared from your life." I grind my jaw, the muscles in my face tightening. "But I couldn't. The thought of not having you was worse than anything I could imagine. So I pursued you, while I kept the truth about your father to myself."

Aurora nods slowly, her shoulders losing some of their rigid tension. The fury in her eyes has dimmed to something quieter but no less painful—a deep, aching wound that I inflicted through my silence.

"I understand why you hate me," I say, keeping my distance despite every instinct to reach for her. "I hate myself for it too."

She wraps her arms around herself, a protective gesture that breaks something inside me.

"I'm not saying I would have expected you to tell me immediately. We barely knew each other." Her voice is soft but steady. "But after everything between us... after I gave you parts of myself..."

"I know." The weight of my betrayal hangs heavy between us. "I told myself I was protecting you. That learning the truth would only cause you pain. But that was a lie I created to justify my cowardice."

A tear slips down her cheek, and she wipes it away quickly, not wanting to show weakness.

"I won't make excuses. There aren't any that matter." I

step back, giving her the physical space that mirrors the emotional distance she needs. "I'm sorry, Aurora. Not just for keeping the truth from you, but for everything Jax has put you through because of me."

She looks up, those azure eyes holding mine. Not with forgiveness—we're nowhere near that shore—but with something like recognition. Of my regret. Of my truth.

"I'll give you the space you need," I continue, my voice rough with emotion I've never allowed myself to express before. "Take whatever time you require. My resources are yours to use in finding Olivia—no strings, no expectations."

I turn to leave, pausing. "I hope someday you find a way to forgive me. Not because I deserve it, but because you deserve peace. And if that means never seeing me again after we find your sister, I'll respect that choice."

I turn and walk away from her, each step heavier than the last.

This unfamiliar pressure builds in my chest, crushing and splitting open something I've kept sealed away my entire life. The sensation is physical—a tearing, a ripping, a violent extraction of something vital I never acknowledged was there.

I've broken men. I've destroyed lives. I've watched the light fade from enemies' eyes without blinking. Hell, I've enjoyed it, the rush of taking a life. Throughout it all, I believed nothing could touch me—that I was constructed differently, immune to the weaknesses of ordinary men.

Yet here I am, thirty-three years of calculated control, crumbling from the inside out.

The hallway stretches endlessly before me. My lungs refuse to work properly. My throat constricts around unspoken words. This is what drowning must feel like—

fighting against something invisible yet absolutely overwhelming.

I press my palm against the wall to steady myself, the brief flash of pain from my injured shoulder almost welcome—a distraction from this new, unbearable hollowness. For the first time in my life, I understand those poetic descriptions of heartbreak. It's not metaphorical. The physical sensation is devastatingly real.

Aurora Harrison. The woman who showed me I had a heart by teaching me what it feels like to have it ripped out.

I force myself forward. One foot. Then the other. My body moving while something essential remains behind with her.

Such a simple offer—to respect her choice if she never wants to see me again. The words came easily. The reality of it guts me completely.

The realization hits like a bullet to the chest: I love her. Not want. Not possess. Not control.

Love.

And I might have lost her forever.

19

AURORA

I wake to the sound of rain against the windows, disoriented for a moment before remembering where I am—Hunter's safe house in the mountains. The digital clock glows 7:23 PM. I've slept longer than I meant to when I laid down for a nap.

For three days, Hunter has given me space while somehow always being present. He brings me meals, sits across from me while I pick at the food, and answers every question I throw at him without hesitation or deflection. No matter how painful or accusatory.

"Your father was a good man," he told me yesterday. "He didn't deserve what happened to him. And you didn't deserve to believe he abandoned you."

I pull myself up from the bed, wrapping the soft blanket around my shoulders. My anger hasn't disappeared—it's transformed into something more complex. A deep ache that acknowledges the truth: while Hunter knew about my father, he was twenty-one himself when it happened, trapped in Jax's web.

The man who's been caring for me these past days isn't

the unfeeling billionaire I first met on that cliff edge. He's someone who finally chose to break free of his chains, risking everything he built to find me. To save me. I think of the bullet wound in his shoulder that he barely acknowledges.

"I won't ask your forgiveness," he said last night, setting down a cup of tea beside me. "I don't deserve it. But I will find Olivia, Aurora. I swear it."

I've been processing not just my father's death but the truth about Hunter. A man capable of terrible things, yet who looks at me with such tenderness it makes my chest ache.

I pad barefoot across the cool wooden floor. The house is quiet except for the distant sound of someone typing. I follow it, blanket trailing behind me like a cape, determined to find him.

It's time we talked about what happens next.

I follow the sound of typing toward the back of the house, but it stops suddenly. The double doors to the library stand partially open, spilling golden light into the darkened hallway. I pause at the threshold, my blanket clutched around my shoulders.

Hunter sits on the leather couch, his laptop abandoned on the coffee table. He's not typing anymore. He's not doing anything at all—just staring straight ahead at the wall of books, his expression haunted. The bandage on his shoulder is visible beneath his thin t-shirt, a reminder of what he risked to find me.

Three empty coffee cups sit on the table. Maps and printouts are scattered across every surface. He hasn't been sleeping while I've been recuperating.

I step into the room, my bare feet silent against the

hardwood. He doesn't notice me until I'm almost beside him.

His eyes snap to mine, instantly alert despite the exhaustion etched into his face and the dark circles around his eyes. The hard edges I've always associated with Hunter Reed seem worn down.

"You should be resting," he says, his voice hoarse.

I ignore his comment and sit beside him on the couch, tucking my legs underneath me, keeping the blanket wrapped around my body like armor.

"What are you thinking?" I ask softly.

Hunter's gaze drops to his hands. They're clasped together so tightly his knuckles have turned white.

"That I don't deserve you," he says quietly. "That whatever happens next, I'm grateful I got to know you at all."

The simple honesty in his words catches me off guard. This isn't the calculating and dominant man who orchestrated his way into my life. This is a man laying himself bare, expecting nothing in return.

I study his profile in the soft lamplight, seeing for the first time how much this has cost him. Not just physically, but something deeper—as if the foundations of his entire existence have shifted.

I reach for Hunter's hand. His eyes follow the movement, wary and uncertain—an expression I've never seen on him before. For a man who's always been so sure of himself, so dominating and in control, this vulnerability is striking.

"Hunter," I whisper, taking his large hand in mine. I place his palm against my chest, pressing it firmly over my heart. Even through the blanket, I can feel the warmth of his skin, the slight tremor in his fingers. "Feel that? It's yours. It has been since we met on that cliff, even when I hated you. Maybe especially then."

His eyes darken, shifting from uncertainty to hunger. The tension between us changes instantly, charging the air with electricity.

"Aurora," he breathes, my name a prayer and a plea.

Hunter pulls me close, nearly crushing me against his chest. I let the blanket fall away as I melt into him. We hold each other in the darkness of the library, the rain still pattering against the windows, creating a cocoon around us. The steady beat of his heart matches mine—quick, desperate.

My fingers thread through his hair as his mouth finds my neck. The anger that burned inside me for days hasn't disappeared, but it's transformed into something equally powerful. I'm starving for him, for this connection that defies all logic. My body remembers his touch even as my mind grapples with everything I've learned.

"I need you," I whisper against his ear, feeling him shudder beneath my hands. "Even when I was so angry I couldn't see straight, I needed you."

His hands slip beneath my shirt, his touch soft and hungry at once. Every point of contact between us sparks with heat, with promise.

His mouth is hot against my skin, desperate. I push away from him suddenly, my palm flat against his chest. Our breathing fills the quiet room, heavy and uneven.

"This doesn't mean I forgive you," I say, my voice sharp and clear. "Don't think for one second that this means everything's okay between us."

Hunter's gray-blue eyes harden, then soften. "I know."

"You let me believe a lie." The words tear from my throat, raw and painful.

I straddle him in one fluid movement, pinning him against the couch. My hands grip his wrists, pressing them into the leather on either side of his head.

"I should hate you," I whisper against his mouth, biting his lower lip hard enough to draw blood. "Part of me still does."

I grind against him, feeling his hardness between my legs. The thin fabric of my sleep shorts and his sweatpants does nothing to disguise how much he wants this—wants me.

"You're going to let me take exactly what I need," I state, releasing one of his wrists to tear at his shirt. "And you're going to give me everything I ask for. Understand?"

"Anything," he breathes, his eyes never leaving mine. "I'll do anything to earn your trust back, Aurora. Anything you want."

I grab his jaw roughly, forcing him to look at me as I roll my hips against his erection. "I want to feel you inside me while I remember exactly who you are—what you've done. I want to come on your cock while I'm still fucking furious with you."

A groan escapes him as I reach between us, shoving his sweatpants down enough to free him.

"You don't deserve this," I whisper, positioning myself above him. "You don't deserve me."

"I know," Hunter says, his voice breaking. "I'll spend the rest of my life trying to be worthy of you."

I position myself above his hard length, my thighs trembling with anticipation. Without warning or gentleness, I sink down on him, taking him to the hilt in one rough motion. The sudden fullness makes me gasp, the delicious stretch burning in all the right ways.

"Touch my clit," I demand, voice tight as I begin to move. "Make me come while I use you."

Hunter's fingers find me immediately, his touch expert and precise. I rock against him hard, setting a punishing pace that has us both panting. My anger fuels every movement, transforming into something primal.

"Harder," I hiss, grinding down on him. "Faster."

He increases the pressure how I need it, his eyes never leaving mine. The intensity between us is electric, charged with everything unsaid. I take my pleasure from him ruthlessly, using his body for my release.

When Hunter's hands suddenly move to grip my hips, I slap them away with a sharp crack.

"No," I snap. "You don't get to touch me however you want. Not anymore." I grab his wrist and place his hand back between my legs. "Fingers on my clit, and one on my nipple. That's it."

He groans, a deep sound of both frustration and arousal. "Aurora—"

"No talking either," I cut him off, rolling my hips in a way that makes us both gasp. "Just do what I tell you."

Hunter obeys, his thumb circling my clit while his other hand reaches up to pinch my nipple through my thin shirt. The dual sensation sends sparks of pleasure shooting through my body. I control everything—the angle, the depth, the pace. His body is mine to use, his pleasure secondary to my own.

I ride him hard, my nails digging into his chest for leverage. Every thrust is an accusation, every moan a confession. I hate him. I want him. I can't live without him. The contradictions tear through me as I chase my release.

I grind against him harder, watching his face contort with pleasure beneath me. There's something intoxicating about seeing this man—this controlling, powerful billionaire who's orchestrated his every move since meeting me—completely at my mercy. Following my commands without question. Taking what I give him.

"Look at you," I whisper, voice sharp with anger and desire. "Hunter Reed, doing exactly what he's told."

His eyes darken at my taunt, but he doesn't speak. Doesn't try to take control. Just continues the relentless rhythm with his fingers that's driving me toward the edge.

And God, I hate how good he makes me feel even while I'm furious with him. How can I crave someone who kept such a devastating truth from me or who is capable of such darkness?

My anger begins to dissolve as the pleasure builds inside me. My hips stutter in their rhythm as Hunter's fingers work their magic, precise and perfect against my clit.

"I hate that I need you like this," I gasp, feeling my body tightening around him. "I hate that even when I'm furious, you still make me feel so fucking good."

His eyes lock with mine, stormy with emotion. I want to look away, but can't. The connection between us transcends the physical—it always has.

"Fuck," I moan, grinding harder against him. "I'm close."

Hunter breaks my rule about silence. "Come for me, Aurora," he whispers, his voice rough. "Give me everything."

Something about those words shatters my remaining control. My orgasm crashes through me in waves, each one more intense than the last. I cry out his name as my body convulses around him, my hands gripping his shoulders despite my earlier command.

Through the haze of my release, I feel Hunter's restraint breaking. His hips thrust up to meet mine, his hands moving to grip my waist. This time, I don't stop him. I need to feel his strength, his desperation.

"I want you to come inside me," I demand, my voice breathy and raw. "Now."

Hunter groans, his fingers digging into my flesh as he thrusts deeper. I feel him pulse inside me, filling me completely as he comes with my name on his lips.

We collapse against each other, panting and sweaty. I rest my head against his shoulder, inhaling his scent. My body feels boneless, satisfied in ways only he can provide.

Despite the lies, despite the pain, I know the truth that terrifies me most: I love him. The realization sits heavy in my chest as I listen to his heartbeat gradually slow. My anger still exists—a burning ember rather than the raging bonfire from before—but it's tangled with something deeper, something I can't deny.

I close my eyes, letting the post-orgasmic haze wash over me. We're far from fixed, but in this moment, I can admit to myself what I've known all along. Hunter Reed and I are like dark and light; neither can exist without the other.

20

HUNTER

I slam my fist on the table, the impact sending three coffee cups rattling. "Nothing. Fucking nothing again."

The satellite image of Jax's supposed Cayman Island property mocks me from the screen—another dead end. Every hour that passes with Olivia in Jax's hands puts Aurora one step closer to hating me all over again. Not that I blame her. I kept secrets about her father's death, and now I can't even deliver on my promise to find Olivia.

"We'll find her, Hunt." Penn leans against the window, his usually carefree demeanor replaced with grim determination. "Jax is good, but he's not a ghost."

Blaze cleans his handgun at the end of the table. "I'd say he's moved her at least four times based on his pattern. Classic evasion technique." His hands never falter in their work. "But everyone makes mistakes eventually."

"Eventually isn't good enough," Ari snaps, pacing like a caged animal. Dark circles shadow his eyes, his perfect appearance uncharacteristically disheveled. "It's been seventeen days. Seventeen fucking days with that psychopath."

Grayson looks up from his laptop. "The Macao lead is still promising. My contact confirmed unusual activity at the property."

"Like the 'unusual activity' in Barbados?" Ari's voice cuts through the room. "Or the warehouse in Manhattan? Or the fucking ski lodge in Vermont?"

I study Ari's face, seeing something I hadn't noticed before—raw desperation beyond loyalty to the mission. "You and Olivia." It's not a question. "While I was with Aurora, you two were—"

"Yes." Ari stops pacing, challenging me with his stare. "We were. And before you start with the *she was my fiancée* bullshit, we both know that was nothing but a business arrangement."

Penn whistles low. "Well, fucking hell. The plot thickens."

"Shut up, Penn," Ari and I say simultaneously.

"How long?" I ask, feeling a strange twist of guilt. While I'd been obsessing over Aurora, I'd barely spared a thought for Olivia beyond her being an obstacle.

"Long enough that I'll burn down every safe house Jax has to get her back," Ari says, his knuckles white as he grips the back of a chair.

I study Ari's face more carefully. The tightly controlled facade he's known for is cracking—eyes too wide, jaw too tight. His perfectly manicured nails dig into the expensive leather of the chair. I recognize that look. It's the same one I saw in the mirror when Aurora was taken.

"You're off this operation," I say, my voice leaving no room for debate.

Ari's head snaps up. "Like hell I am."

"You're compromised. Emotions make you sloppy, and sloppy gets people killed." I tap the table, emphasizing each word. "Or have you forgotten how I nearly got everyone killed at the warehouse because I couldn't think straight?"

"That's different," Ari snarls.

Penn snorts. "How exactly is it different? Because it's you instead of Hunter?"

"Because we're wasting time with this intelligence bullshit!" Ari sweeps his arm across the table, sending papers flying. "Jax isn't in fucking Macao or the Caymans. He's at the Montana compound."

Blaze stops cleaning his weapon. "Montana was cleared three days ago."

"The official compound was cleared," Ari says, his voice dropping dangerously. "Not the hunting lodge. Somewhere within a ten miles radius, accessible only by helicopter or a maintenance road that doesn't appear on any map. Jax mentioned it once, years ago. Said it was where he'd go if things went sideways."

Grayson's fingers fly across his keyboard. "There's nothing in our files about a secondary location in Montana."

"Because Jax wouldn't put it in the files," Ari says, exasperated. "You think he hasn't been planning for this possibility for years? He's paranoid enough to have places we don't know about."

I narrow my eyes. "And you conveniently remember this now?"

"I didn't remember until—" Ari stops, running his hand through his hair. "Look, I had a dream last night. About something Jax said years ago at that ski trip in Aspen. About having a place where no one could find him. A place with no digital footprint not far from the official compound in Montana."

"Not far? That's it? That's what you're going with?" I shake my head at Ari. "So what, we just go and sweep an entire huge area of wilderness based on something you vaguely remember from a dream?"

"It's not just a dream. It was a real conversation," Ari insists, his knuckles white against the chair.

"You're not thinking straight," I say, echoing the same words I'd used for myself days earlier. "We can't divert resources based on a hunch or some unverified piece of information you half-remembered. We need concrete intel."

"Fuck you," Ari snarls, shoving the chair. "Every minute we waste, she's with him. Every fucking minute."

He storms toward the door, slamming it hard enough to rattle the hinges.

Penn sighs, shaking his head. "He's lost it. Completely fucking lost it. We can't search hundreds of square miles of Montana wilderness on a dream."

"But what if he's right?" Blaze asks quietly. "What if she is there?"

Grayson looks up from his computer. "It's a long shot. But Jax is theatrical enough to hide in plain sight. I'm not saying to commit everything, but..." He trails off, clearly conflicted.

I close my eyes, seeing Aurora's face. If Olivia is somewhere in those mountains with Jax, and we miss her because I dismissed Ari's instinct... Aurora would never forgive me. Hell, I'd never forgive myself.

But we have no solid intel. No satellite confirmation. Nothing concrete to go on.

"Send drones," I say finally. "Catalog every structure

within a ten-mile radius of the Montana compound. Every cabin, hunting blind, and outbuilding. If there's a secondary location, we'll find it."

Grayson nods, already typing commands into his laptop. Penn and Blaze exchange a look before gathering their things. I can read their skepticism, but they're loyal. They'll execute the order regardless.

"I'll coordinate with our team on the ground," Penn says, heading for the door.

Blaze follows, silently sliding his reassembled weapon into his holster.

As they file out, I turn toward the window, my shoulders tight with fatigue. A soft intake of breath from the other side of the room alerts me to another presence. Aurora stands in the second doorway, her arms wrapped around herself, dark hair falling loose around her shoulders. How long has she been there?

"Do you think she's there?" Aurora asks, her voice surprisingly steady despite the dark circles under her eyes. "In Montana?"

I want to lie, to give her hope, but I've done enough damage with deception. "I don't know," I admit, running a hand through my hair. "Ari could be right, or it could be desperation talking. He and Olivia were... involved."

Aurora nods slowly. "I know. She told me, back in the cell."

"The Vipers have safe houses all over North America. Properties that don't officially exist." I step toward her, keeping my distance but needing to be closer. "Some only Jax knows about. Montana is just one possibility among dozens."

"But you're looking," she says, a statement rather than a question.

"We're looking everywhere. I won't stop until we find her." I meet her eyes directly. "I won't leave any stone unturned, Aurora. I'll do anything to make things right with you. And I will do anything to bring your sister home."

Aurora perches on the edge of the table. Her eyes meet mine, something softer in them than I've seen since her rescue.

"I've been thinking," she says quietly. "About everything with my father. With us."

I stay silent, giving her the space to continue. These moments when she opens up feel like walking on glass—one wrong move and everything shatters.

"We hadn't known each other that long, had we? Before all this happened." She tucks her hair behind her ear. "A few weeks. Some intense moments. It wasn't like we'd built the kind of relationship where I should expect you to just... blurt out something like that."

I lean against the wall, keeping my distance. "I wanted to tell you. I just—"

"I know." She cuts me off with a small gesture. "That's what I'm trying to say. I reacted so strongly because..." Her voice catches. "For twelve years, I thought my father chose to leave me. That he looked at his life—at me and my mom—and decided we weren't enough reason to stay."

A single tear slides down her cheek.

"I've been so angry at him, Hunter. So fucking angry. For abandoning us. For being selfish. I built my entire understanding of love and trust around the fact that my father chose to die rather than stay with us. Hell, I even took Derek's second name almost to spite him, which is ridiculous because he's dead, and..." She looks up at the ceiling, blinking rapidly. "And then to find out he was murdered? That he didn't choose to leave us at all?" Her voice breaks. "It was like my heart was being torn out all over again. Everything I thought I knew about that day, about him, about myself... it all changed in an instant."

I watch her carefully, recognizing the grief etched in every line of her body.

"I needed someone to blame," she admits softly. "And you were there."

I cross the room without thinking, closing the distance between us in four strides. My hands cup her face, thumbs brushing away the tears that follow the first. For once in my life, I don't calculate my next move. I just need to hold her.

"Aurora," I whisper, pressing my forehead against hers. "I should have told you everything from the start." My voice roughens. "From this moment on, no more secrets. I swear it. Anything you want to know—anything at all—I'll tell you."

Her hands rest against my chest, not pushing away, not pulling closer. Just feeling my heartbeat.

"When Jax took you..." My throat tightens around the words. "I couldn't sleep. Couldn't eat. For the first time in my life, I was completely out of control." I close my eyes. "I can't function without you. I've spent my entire life not needing anyone, and now I can't breathe when you're not here."

Her fingers curl into my shirt. "Hunter..."

"I love you." The words I've never said to another living soul come out with startling ease. "Not just want. Not just need. I love you, Aurora."

She rises on her toes and presses her lips to mine. Gentle at first, then hungrier, more desperate. I lift her onto the table, maps and satellite photos scattering beneath her. She pulls me closer, her legs wrapping around my waist.

"Show me," she whispers against my mouth. "Show me how much."

I sweep the remaining papers to the floor with one arm, laying her back against the polished wood. My hands find the hem of her shirt, sliding underneath to feel her warm skin. Every touch is a promise. Every kiss a vow.

Her fingers work at my belt, urgent and demanding. When I hesitate, her eyes lock with mine.

"I need you," she says simply. "Now."

Nothing else matters—not Jax, not Olivia, not the Vipers. Just Aurora beneath me on the table where minutes ago I'd been planning war, her body arching into mine as I claim her mouth again.

I pin her wrists above her head with one hand. Her surrender—this beautiful, fierce woman willingly giving herself to me—ignites something primal in my chest.

"Look at you," I murmur, my free hand sliding her shirt higher. "So fucking perfect. All mine."

Her eyes flutter closed as I lower my mouth to her exposed stomach, tasting the salt of her skin. My teeth graze over her ribs, making her arch against my hold.

"Hunter, please," she whispers, straining against my grip.

"Stay still," I command, tightening my fingers around her wrists. "Let me have you. Let go, Aurora."

The subtle yielding in her body sends heat coursing through my veins.

"That's it," I praise, dragging my tongue along the underside of her breast. "Give yourself to me, beautiful girl."

I press my hardness against her center, still clothed but unmistakable. Her breath catches when I rock against her, the friction making her whimper.

"You're going to take me right here," I growl against her throat, my teeth finding the tender spot where her pulse hammers. "Going to spread those gorgeous legs and let me inside that perfect cunt."

But even as the filthy words leave my mouth, I'm pressing kisses against her jaw, her temple, the corner of her eye. Gentle in contrast to my crude promises.

"I've dreamed of this every night since you were taken," I confess, undoing her jeans with one hand. "Not just fucking you. Worshipping every goddamn inch of you."

Her eyes open at that, meeting mine with something vulnerable in their depths.

"No one else gets to see you like this," I murmur, sliding her pants down her thighs. "Just me. My Aurora, my heart. My perfect fucking goddess."

The tenderness in my voice surprises even me, woven between filthy promises that make her breath hitch. But I mean every word—the crude demands and the reverent praise alike.

"I'm going to ruin you for anyone else," I tell her, releasing her wrists to shed my own clothes. "And then I'm going to put you back together with my hands, my mouth, my cock."

Aurora reaches for me, pulling me down to her with surprising strength. Her eyes—those impossibly blue eyes that have haunted me since the first moment I saw her on that cliff—lock with mine.

"I love you," she whispers, her voice breaking with emotion. "Every dark, twisted part of you. The monster and the man. All of you, Hunter."

A dam I've built over decades crumbles in seconds. I capture her mouth in a bruising kiss, swallowing her gasp as I push her thighs wider.

"Say it again," I demand, my voice barely recognizable.

Her fingers dig into my shoulders. "I love you," she breathes against my lips. "The darkness in you calls to mine. I love all of it—the violence, the possessiveness, the need to control."

I growl low in my throat, lifting her hips to position her at the edge of the table. "You have no idea what you're doing to me."

"Show me," she challenges, wrapping her legs around my waist. "Don't hold back. I'm not fragile."

When I thrust into her, it's without gentleness—claiming, marking, branding her as mine. She cries out, her back arching off the table, but her nails digging deeper tell me she wants this just as rough as I need to give it.

"Mine," I snarl against her throat, setting a punishing pace.

"Yours," she agrees, meeting each thrust. "Always yours."

Even in this storm of possession and need, I find myself pressing tender kisses to her temple, her cheek. My hands grip her with such force, but my thumbs stroke softly against her skin. Violence and tenderness twined together —just like us.

"I never thought I could feel this," I confess against her ear. "Never thought I was capable—"

"You are," she interrupts, framing my face with her hands. "With me, you are."

I drive into her with renewed force. The table creaks beneath us as I pound into her, claiming every inch of her body.

"Fuck, Aurora," I growl, my control slipping completely. "I want to fill you up. Want you pregnant with my child."

Her eyes widen, pupils blown with desire.

"You'd look so fucking perfect," I continue, voice rough as I slam into her. "Swollen with my baby. Everyone would know you're mine. Completely fucking mine."

Aurora moans, her inner walls clenching around me. I grab her ass, tilting her hips to hit deeper.

"Tell me you want it," I demand, sweat dripping down my back as I thrust harder. "Tell me you want me to breed you."

"Yes," she gasps, her nails drawing blood on my shoulders. "Fill me up, Hunter. I want it. Want you."

I lose myself in her completely, fucking her with animal intensity. The slap of skin against skin echoes through the room as I pound into her relentlessly.

"Going to come inside you," I growl against her ear. "Going to put my baby in you."

Her body tenses, back arching off the table as she screams my name. I feel the rush of wetness as she squirts around my cock, the sensation pushing me over the edge. I bury myself to the hilt and roar as I come, emptying everything I have inside her.

We stay joined, her legs still wrapped around my waist, both of us panting. The intensity slowly melts into something softer as I press lazy kisses along her jaw, her cheeks, her eyelids. She sighs contentedly, fingers threading through my hair.

"Stay," she whispers, tightening around me when I shift slightly.

I have no desire to move, to break this connection. I lean down to kiss her slowly, deeply, our bodies still joined intimately.

21

AURORA

My body is pleasantly sore in a way that brings a flush to my cheeks as memories of last night flood back. The sunlight streaming through the windows casts a golden hue over everything. Hunter's arm is heavy across my waist, possessive even in sleep. For a moment, I allow myself to feel safe.

But reality crashes back quickly. Liv is still missing. Jax still has her. And we're no closer to finding them.

Hunter stirs beside me, instantly alert in that unnerving way of his. His hand slides up my bare back. "Morning," he murmurs against my hair.

"Morning," I reply, turning onto my side to face him. "Any news?"

He shakes his head. "Drones are still searching the Montana area. We should know something by this afternoon."

I nod, swallowing my disappointment. Every hour Liv spends with Jax feels like an eternity.

"I think it's safe for us to head back to the city today," Hunter says, sitting up. "I've had the penthouse swept for bugs, and security's been doubled. There are men stationed in the lobby now too."

My stomach tightens. "I don't know if I can go back to the city without her."

"We'll find her," he promises, the certainty in his voice almost convincing me.

"Have you..." I hesitate, "Have you spoken to my dad about all this?"

Hunter's expression shifts subtly. "Yes. He's helping with resources, information. He's understandably upset about what's happened."

"Did you tell him about us?" The question comes out smaller than I intended.

Hunter's fingers brush my cheek. "Not yet. It didn't seem like the right time, finding out you'd both been kidnapped. He's focused on finding Olivia."

I nod, understanding his reasoning even as I wonder how my father will react when he does find out. His stepdaughter and his daughter's fiancé. It sounds like the plot of a bad soap opera.

"We'll tell him," Hunter says, reading my thoughts. "Together. Hopefully after we bring Olivia home, unless we need to tell him sooner."

"But what do I tell him when he asks where I'm staying? Because he will ask." I twist the bedsheet between my fingers. "I can't exactly say I'm living with his business partner, who is, as far as he's concerned, still engaged to his daughter."

Hunter's expression doesn't change as he traces patterns on my bare shoulder. "You don't tell him anything. He doesn't need to know where you're staying."

"But—"

"I've already spoken to Derek about your security,"

Hunter interrupts. "I assured him I'd find secure accommodation for you, under protection. He was satisfied with that."

I raise an eyebrow. "And he didn't ask for details?"

"He tried. I explained that the fewer people who knew your location, the safer you'd be." Hunter's lips quirk into a half-smile. "Your father understands security is paramount."

I nod, releasing a deep sigh. Part of me wants to come clean immediately and stop living in the shadows. But another part recognizes Hunter's logic. With Jax still out there and Liv by missing, maybe complete honesty isn't the priority right now.

"Come on." Hunter slides from the bed, pulling on a pair of sweatpants that hang dangerously low on his hips. "Let's get some food."

I watch him move toward the door, all lean muscle and predatory grace. "I didn't know you could cook."

He glances back, something almost playful crossing his features. "There are still a few things you don't know about me, Aurora."

In the kitchen, I perch on a barstool while Hunter moves with surprising efficiency, cracking eggs into a bowl, slicing bread, and measuring coffee grounds. The domesticity of the moment feels surreal after everything we've been through.

"How did you learn to cook?" I ask as he whisks the eggs with practiced movements.

"Necessity." He doesn't look up from his task. "When you grow up without parents, you either learn or starve."

The simple statement catches me off guard, a reminder of the layers still between us. I don't know a lot about him or his past. I watch silently as he pours the eggs into a sizzling pan, thinking about all the questions I still need to ask him.

I watch him move around the kitchen with practiced ease, the revelation about his childhood hanging in the air between us. The question forms before I can stop it.

"Why did you grow up without parents? What happened to them?"

Hunter's hands pause momentarily over the stove. His shoulders tense, and I immediately regret asking.

"I'm sorry. You don't have to—"

"No," he interrupts, his voice uncharacteristically soft. "You should know." He flips the eggs onto plates and turns off the burner before meeting my eyes. "Car accident. I was seven."

The simple statement lands with crushing weight. I remain silent, giving him space to continue or stop.

Hunter places the plates on the counter and leans against it, eyes fixed on some distant point. "Rainy night. Drunk driver. They were coming home from a charity event while I was being watched by the babysitter." His voice is methodical, as if reciting facts from a report, but I can see the muscle in his jaw working.

"I'm so sorry," I whisper.

"My uncle took me in afterward." A bitter smile crosses his face. "Not out of familial love. My parents left everything to me in a trust. He wanted control of it."

"That's horrible."

Hunter shrugs. "He provided a roof. Food. Private schools to keep me out of his way. Otherwise, I barely existed." His eyes finally meet mine. "I learned to cook because he fired the staff who showed me kindness. But a few maids took pity on me anyway. Taught me things when he wasn't around."

I slide off my stool and move to him, placing my hand over his. "That must have been incredibly lonely."

"I adapted." His fingers intertwine with mine. "I built my own life. My own family with the Vipers."

The pain beneath his controlled exterior makes my heart ache. I understand better now—why control matters so much to him, why he holds people at a distance.

"Thank you," I say quietly. "For telling me."

Hunter's gaze softens, and in that moment, I glimpse the child he once was—abandoned, determined to never need anyone again.

I step closer to him, placing my palm against his cheek. The man who terrifies enemies and commands empires leans into my touch like he's starved for it.

"You know you don't have to be alone anymore," I whisper. "Not ever again."

"Aurora..."

"I mean it," I continue, my thumb tracing his jawline. "I know we've been through hell, and there's still so much ahead of us, but whatever comes next, we will face it together."

Hunter pulls me against him, burying his face in my hair. I feel him trembling, his breath uneven against my neck. When he lifts his head, I'm stunned to see moisture in his eyes.

"Hunter," I breathe, reaching up to touch a tear tracking down his cheek.

He catches my hand, looking almost surprised at the wetness on his own fingers. "I haven't cried since I was a kid," he admits. "Not since the funeral."

I rise on my toes and kiss him softly, our lips barely touching—so different from our usual desperate hunger.

This kiss feels like a promise, tender in ways neither of us is accustomed to giving or receiving.

When I pull back, another tear has escaped. I brush it away and find myself smiling. "Look at that. The great Hunter Reed, brought down by a few childhood stories and a kiss."

A low chuckle rumbles through his chest. "Careful," he warns, though his eyes remain soft. "People might think you're melting all that ice around my heart."

"Good," I say, pressing another kiss to the corner of his mouth. "It was getting a bit chilly there anyway."

His arms tighten around me as he laughs again—a real laugh that transforms his entire face. "Only you," he murmurs against my temple. "Only you could do this to me."

His arms tighten around me, our forgotten breakfast cooling on the counter. In this moment, with sunlight spilling across the kitchen tiles and the world temporarily held at bay, Hunter's vulnerability strikes me as the most precious gift he could offer.

I rise on my toes again, my hands sliding up to frame his face. His eyes—those blue-gray eyes that have looked at me with lust, possession, even rage—now hold something infinitely more dangerous: trust.

Hunter's hands cradle my face like I'm something precious. His thumbs brush my cheeks as he deepens the kiss with aching slowness. I taste salt from his tears, feel the slight tremble in his fingers.

"I've never let anyone see me like this," he whispers against my lips.

I press closer. "I know."

When he kisses me again, I feel walls crumbling—not just his, but mine too. The barriers we've built around our hearts, the defenses constructed from years of loss and pain, dissolve with each gentle brush of his lips.

His forehead rests against mine, our breathing synchronized. "I meant what I said, Aurora. I love you." He says the words carefully, like they're new tools he's learning to use. "I've never said that to anyone before."

Tears sting my eyes. In all our passionate encounters, in all the possessive words he's growled against my skin, nothing has ever made me feel more his than this moment of quiet confession.

"I love you too," I whisper back, the words carrying the weight of everything we've been through, everything we still face.

His smile—soft and real and just for me—is worth every moment of pain that brought us here.

22

HUNTER

The morning light filters through the penthouse windows as I watch Aurora across the kitchen island. She's stirring her coffee absently, scrolling through news alerts on her tablet. Even in this mundane moment, wearing one of my T-shirts that drowns her slender frame, she's captivating.

Three days of living together since returning from the mountain safehouse, and I'm addicted to these quiet moments. The way she hums in the shower. How she curls against me in sleep. The domesticity of it feels foreign but strangely right.

"Anything?" I ask, knowing she's checking for anything about Liv or Jax.

Aurora shakes her head, the worry etching lines between her brows. "Nothing new."

I circle the island and press my lips to her temple. "The Montana lead is solid. Grayson's team is narrowing the search grid hourly."

She leans into me, her body seeking comfort even as her

mind refuses it. This balance between us is still new—her allowing herself to need me while maintaining her fierce independence. It's a delicate dance we're learning together.

"I know," she says. "I just—"

"We'll find her," I promise, turning her to face me. "Whatever it takes."

Her fingers trace the line of my jaw—a gesture that's become familiar in the past days. These small touches communicate more than words ever could between us.

The security panel by the door chimes, interrupting our moment. The penthouse camera feed shows Grayson standing in the private elevator hallway.

"It's Grayson," I tell Aurora, noting her immediate tension.

I cross to the door, already sensing something's wrong from Grayson's stance. When I open it, my suspicion is confirmed. His normally composed expression is taut, his eyes holding the controlled intensity that only appears when things have gone sideways.

"What happened?" I ask without preamble.

Grayson glances past me to where Aurora stands. His jaw tightens. "We need to talk," he says, his voice deliberately neutral in that way that sends ice through my veins.

"What's wrong?" I demand.

Grayson's eyes dart to Aurora briefly before focusing back on me. "We have a situation."

I step aside, letting him into the penthouse. Aurora approaches, her posture rigid with anticipation. Her hand finds mine, squeezing.

"Tell us," I say, gripping Aurora's hand tighter.

Grayson exhales heavily. "We got a call from Ari about two hours ago. He was in Montana, operating on his own."

"Montana?" Aurora's voice rises. "Where Liv might be?"

Grayson nods grimly. "He found the cabin. Confirmed Jax was holding Olivia there."

"Fuck," I growl. "Why wasn't I notified immediately?"

"Because he went dark afterward. Said he was going in." Grayson's expression hardens. "We begged him to wait, wait for backup, but he didn't listen. He was too emotional about Olivia."

Aurora's fingers dig into my palm. "What happened?"

"We redirected a surveillance drone to his coordinates." Grayson pulls out his tablet, his movements precise, controlled. "We were too late. The footage shows Jax taking Liv and Ari, loading them into an unmarked van."

"Show me," I demand.

Grayson hands me the tablet. The grainy aerial footage shows a remote cabin surrounded by dense forest. Three figures move across the clearing—Jax's tall frame unmistakable even from this distance, a second man dragging what appears to be Ari's unconscious body, and between them, Olivia, her blonde hair catching the sunlight.

I feel Aurora trembling beside me as she watches her sister being forced into a black van that disappears down a dirt road moments later.

"When was this?" I ask, my voice deadly calm.

"Ninety minutes ago."

"Did the drone follow them?" I ask, my voice tight as I hand the tablet back to Grayson.

He nods, rubbing his jaw with tension evident in every movement. "It followed as far as it could, heading south. But then it ran out of battery and had to return to base. Couldn't keep following."

"Fuck." I turn to the window, mind already mapping possibilities. "Traffic cameras? Highway patrol?"

"There's no ANPR in the area," Grayson says. "And they

were sticking to the back roads. Local infrastructure is minimal at best."

Aurora's face drains of color. I watch her hands begin to shake—the same tremor I'd noticed during her first days of recovery. Her eyes fill with tears as she looks between us.

"Does this mean we've lost them forever?" Her voice cracks, raw panic rising. "We were so close! She was right there!" She presses her fist against her mouth, trying to contain a sob. "What if we never find her now?"

I cross to her immediately, taking her face between my hands. "Listen to me. We are going to find them. This isn't over."

"But if you don't know where—"

"We'll know," I say firmly. "Jax can't go far without leaving traces. He's arrogant, thinks he's invincible. That makes him predictable."

Aurora's breathing comes too fast, her chest rising and falling rapidly. I press my forehead to hers, forcing her to focus on me.

"And now Ari is with her," I continue, my voice low and steady. "He's trained for situations like this. He's resourceful, skilled. At the very least, Liv isn't facing this alone anymore."

"You think he can protect her?" Aurora whispers, hope threading through her words.

"I think he'll do anything to keep her safe," I say. "And maybe find a way to get them both out. Jax doesn't know everything about Ari—what he's capable of when pushed."

Aurora nods, her breathing slowing as she clings to this small comfort. "At least she's not alone now."

Grayson takes out his phone, his fingers already tapping commands as he speaks. "I'm getting everyone on this.

Penn's coordinating with our satellite team to scan the area, and Blaze is analyzing the most likely routes based on the drone footage."

I nod, watching him work with the efficiency that's made him invaluable to me for years.

"I've got a ground team deploying to the last known coordinates," he continues, not looking up from his screen. "They'll take the same roads and check every possible turnoff, abandoned structure, and potential hiding place along the route."

"ETA?" I ask, keeping my arm firmly around Aurora's shoulders.

Grayson's expression tightens. "They're about twenty minutes out. It's remote terrain, and our closest operatives were stationed at the perimeter we established. They're moving as fast as possible, but—"

"But Jax has a significant head start," I finish for him.

He nods grimly. "It's going to be tough to find them on the ground alone. But we're not just relying on that. I've got contacts in three state police forces checking in-state cameras. Any vehicle matching that description will trigger an alert."

I move forward and clap Grayson firmly on the shoulder. His loyalty has never wavered, even when following me meant turning against Jax and the Vipers we helped build.

"Thanks," I say simply, the word inadequate for what he's risking.

"When you inevitably get yourself killed," Grayson replies with a hint of his usual dry humor, "I expect a significant raise in your will."

Despite everything, I feel the corner of my mouth lift. "What makes you think you're in it at all?"

Grayson snorts. "Please. Someone has to keep your empire from burning to the ground when you're gone."

I laugh, the sound breaking some of the tension in the room. "Get out of here. And keep me updated every thirty minutes."

Grayson nods, already checking his phone as he heads back toward the elevator. The door slides shut behind him, leaving Aurora and me alone in the sudden silence.

Aurora crosses to the window, wrapping her arms around herself. "What if we don't get another lead, Hunter? What if this was our one chance?"

I approach her carefully, seeing the tremors starting again in her shoulders. "Jax won't disappear completely. He's too arrogant for that."

"You don't understand," she whispers, her voice cracking. She turns to me, tears forming in her eyes. "When we were there... Jax had this—this interest in Liv."

My entire body goes rigid. "What do you mean?"

"Sexual interest." The words fall from her lips like stones. "He would come to our cell, drug me so I couldn't move but could still see, and then—" Her voice breaks. "Then he'd touch her. Make her—"

She can't finish the sentence. She doesn't need to. The implication alone makes my blood turn to ice.

"He was obsessed with her. The way he looked at her..." Aurora's composure finally cracks, her body folding in on itself as sobs wrack her frame. "It was sick. And he still has her."

I pull her against me, cradling her head to my chest while fury burns through every cell in my body. "We'll get her back," I promise, though I know the reality is far more complicated.

If Jax wants Olivia that way—if he's fixated on her—

separating them will be exponentially more difficult. Jax doesn't relinquish what he considers his. Not willingly. Not ever.

And Ari—fucking hell. If he loves Olivia as much as I suspect he does, as much as I've seen in his desperate search for her these past weeks, he'll fight to protect her from Jax's advances. Which puts him in immediate, lethal danger.

Jax won't tolerate competition. Especially not from someone he'll view as a traitor.

I hold Aurora against my chest, her body shaking with sobs as the full horror of what she's revealed sinks in.

The thought of Ari walking into that situation blindly makes my stomach turn. He's skilled, strategic, one of the best—but he didn't know what he was walking into. His judgment would be compromised by his feelings for Olivia. Against a psychopath like Jax, that's deadly.

Without letting go of Aurora, I pull my phone from my pocket and text Grayson:

New intel. Jax has a sexual fixation on Olivia. Was assaulting her while they were captive. Aurora witnessed. Changes threat assessment. Ari is likely to provoke an immediate hostile response if he tries to protect her.

I add after a moment's thought:

And Grayson—make sure the team knows. No holding back when we find them. Jax doesn't walk away from this.

I set the phone down and pull Aurora closer, resting my chin on top of her head. Her tears soak through my shirt as her fingers grip the fabric like she's afraid I'll disappear too.

"Listen to me," I murmur against her hair. "We're going to get them back. Both of them."

Her breathing hitches. "You don't know that."

"I do." My voice hardens with certainty. "And Jax is

going to pay for everything he's done. To your father. To you. To Olivia."

I feel her nod weakly against my chest.

"I will burn the world down to find them," I promise. "And when I do, Jax won't survive what comes next."

23

AURORA

My fingers hover over my phone, a knot forming in my throat as I stare at the screen. Five days back in the city, and I've avoided this call long enough. I press the group chat icon for my friends.

Instantly, messages flood in.

> Daisy: AURORA! Oh my god, where have you been?
>
> Grace: We've been worried sick about you and Liv!
>
> Chloe: Are you okay? No one's telling us anything

I take a deep breath and type.

> I'm safe. I need to see you all. Can you meet at Caffeine & Co near downtown in an hour? I'll explain everything.

Their responses are immediate—they'll all be there.

Hunter wraps his arms around me from behind, his breath warm against my ear. "You sure about this? It might be dangerous."

"They're my friends. I can't keep hiding from them." I turn to face him. "I need something normal right now."

He nods reluctantly. "Marcus will go with you."

"One of your security team?" I ask.

Hunter's jaw tightens. "Marcus is a former special forces soldier. He's good. He'll keep his distance but stay close enough."

An hour later, I'm sitting at a corner table in the café. Marcus, a broad-shouldered man with watchful eyes, positions himself three tables away, his gaze continuously scanning the room.

When my friends burst through the door, their faces a mixture of relief and concern, something inside me breaks, and I start crying. Grace reaches me first, wrapping me in a fierce hug.

"Where have you been?" she whispers. "And where's Liv?"

Daisy and Chloe join the hug, creating a protective circle around me. When we finally separate, tears streak all our faces.

"What happened at that masquerade ball?" Chloe asks, gripping my hand across the table. "One minute you were there, the next you vanished—Olivia too."

I take a deep breath, my hands trembling around my coffee cup. My friends watch me with worried expressions, waiting for answers. Where do I even begin?

"At the masquerade ball," I start, my voice lower than I intended, "Olivia and I were—" I pause, the memory flashing vividly. "We were drugged and kidnapped."

Daisy gasps, her hand flying to her mouth. Chloe's eyes widen in shock, and Grace reaches for my arm.

"By whom?" Grace asks, her voice tight.

"A man named Jax King. He's..." I choose my words carefully, "Hunter's enemy. They have some kind of business rivalry that turned dangerous."

"Oh my god," Chloe whispers.

I fidget with my napkin. "Hunter had been searching for us since that night. He finally found me at a warehouse by the coast, but—" My voice cracks. "By then, Jax had moved Liv somewhere else. He still has her."

"But you're safe now?" Daisy asks, her eyes darting to Marcus, clearly noticing his protective stance.

"Yes. Hunter rescued me about a week ago. I was..." I swallow hard. "I was held captive for almost two weeks."

Grace's grip on my arm tightens. "And Hunter is still looking for Liv?"

"Every resource he has is focused on finding her. We had a lead in Montana, but—" I stop, not wanting to share about Ari being captured too. "It didn't pan out. Jax is always one step ahead."

"Why would someone do this?" Chloe asks, tears welling in her eyes.

"To hurt Hunter," I say simply. "Jax wanted to take something Hunter cared about."

I don't tell them about my father's murder or that Hunter knew all along. I don't mention the Vipers organization or the blood and violence of the past weeks. They don't need that burden. They just need to know enough to understand why I've disappeared and why Olivia is still missing.

I fidget with my coffee cup, the steam rising between us. They need to know the whole truth.

"There's more," I say, my voice barely audible over the

café chatter. "And I need you all to just... listen. Don't judge me until I've finished."

Their expressions shift from concern to wariness.

Daisy reaches for my hand. "Whatever it is, we're here for you," she says softly. I wonder if she suspects what I'll say, considering she knew about our almost kiss.

I take a deep breath. "Hunter and I... we're together. Romantically. It started before the masquerade ball, before the kidnapping."

The silence that follows feels suffocating. Grace's eyebrows shoot up, Chloe's mouth falls open, and Daisy squeezes my hand tighter.

"But he was engaged to Olivia," Grace finally says.

"I know. That's why I said don't judge me until I explain." I stare down at the table. "It was wrong. I betrayed my sister. But the engagement was a business arrangement set up by my step-dad. It wasn't real."

"Does Liv know about you two?" Chloe asks.

I nod. "When we were held captive together, I finally told her everything. I couldn't keep lying to her, especially in that situation." My throat tightens remembering our cell. "She was upset, but not because of Hunter. She was angry that I hadn't been honest with her."

"So she didn't care about Hunter?" Daisy asks.

"No, because—" I push my hair behind my ear, "—she'd been seeing Ari Carter. Hunter's friend. They'd been together about the same time."

"Ari Carter?" Grace asks, clearly shocked. "The guy who's always at those charity events?"

I nod. "Hunter and I weren't the only ones with secrets."

"So this whole time, you were with Hunter, and Liv was

with Ari, while everyone thought Hunter and Liv were engaged?" Chloe summarizes, her eyes wide.

"Yes. And now Jax has Liv." I blink back tears. "I'm terrified for them. And I feel responsible. If I hadn't gotten involved with Hunter..." My voice trails off, the weight of guilt pressing down.

Daisy shakes her head firmly. "Aurora, you can't blame yourself."

"Then this probably still would have happened, because this enemy wanted to hurt him, right?" I admit, twisting a napkin between my fingers. "Jax was already watching Hunter. He might have taken Olivia anyway, just because she was Hunter's fiancée."

No one speaks for a long moment. The café bustles around us, people living normal lives, ordering coffee, laughing about weekend plans. The contrast with our reality feels surreal.

Chloe clears her throat. "So... does Hunter have, like, a team of super hot Jason Bourne types looking for Liv? Because that would explain Muscles McGee over there." She tilts her head subtly toward Marcus.

The unexpected comment startles a laugh out of me. "Something like that."

"I knew rich people had their secrets, but this is some next-level shit," Grace says, attempting a smile. "Like, what's next? Does Ari have a secret lair? Does Daisy's crush have a double life as an international spy?"

Daisy blushes furiously. "I don't have a crush."

"You absolutely do," Chloe counters, momentarily slipping into our normal banter. "You've been stalking Penn's Instagram for months."

For a fleeting moment, it feels like before—the four of

us sharing secrets, teasing each other. Then reality crashes back.

"Fuck," Chloe whispers, her smile fading. "I can't believe Liv is kidnapped by a psycho right now."

"I know," Grace murmurs, reaching for my hand.

"It doesn't feel real," Daisy adds, eyes glistening.

I look at my friends' troubled faces and realize I need to give us all a moment of normalcy—something that doesn't involve kidnapping or secret relationships or life-threatening danger. Even if it feels forced, we need this.

"Let's talk about something else," I say, straightening in my seat. "I've been locked away from the world. What's been happening with you all? What did I miss? Please—I need to hear about normal life."

They exchange uncertain glances, clearly caught off guard by the shift.

"It feels wrong to talk about our boring lives when Liv is..." Grace trails off, but I shake my head.

"No, I need this. Just for a few minutes. Please."

Chloe, always quick to adapt, nods enthusiastically. "Well, I finally got that promotion at the museum. Senior curator."

"That's amazing," I say, forcing a smile that gradually becomes more genuine. "You've been working toward that for so long."

"And I met someone," Daisy says quietly, a faint blush coloring her cheeks. "Nothing serious yet, but... he's interesting."

"Not Penn, I assume?" I tease gently, remembering Chloe's comment earlier.

Daisy's blush deepens. "No. His name is James. He's a lawyer with that firm downtown."

"She's being modest," Grace cuts in. "He's absolutely

smitten with her. He sends flowers to her office every week."

For a brief moment, the tension in the air lifts. We're just four friends catching up, sharing life updates.

"What about you, Grace?" I ask. "Any news?"

She hesitates, then shrugs. "The gallery's been getting offers from some corporate buyer. He keeps raising the price. I keep saying no."

"Xavier Porter's company," Chloe supplies. "Grace hates him."

"I don't hate him," Grace protests. "I just don't trust him. There's something off about a tech bro suddenly interested in art."

As I listen to Grace talk about her gallery troubles, I find myself clinging to her words like a lifeline. This normal conversation—this mundane evening with friends—keeps the darker thoughts at bay, if only for moments at a time.

But they creep back in, unwelcome and persistent.

What is Liv enduring right now? Is she scared? Hurt? The image of her with Jax flashes through my mind—her back arching, her lips parting in what looked like pleasure, not pain. My stomach churns with dread.

You belong to me now, don't you, Olivia?

Yes... I belong to you.

I blink hard, trying to erase the memory. What if she wasn't just playing along to survive? What if something in her actually responded to him? The thought makes me physically ill, but I can't deny what I saw with my own eyes.

Maybe it was just survival. Maybe it was Stockholm syndrome. Or maybe there was something darker in my sister that Jax recognized and drew out.

I take another sip of my coffee, forcing myself to focus on Chloe's animated hand gestures as she describes some gallery mishap. Meanwhile, I'm sitting here, safe with our friends. Protected. Sleeping in Hunter's penthouse at night with its ridiculous thread-count sheets and panoramic views. I have security. Comfort. The man I love.

And Liv has... what? A monster? A cell? Or worse—what if she's developing feelings for her captor?

The guilt is crushing. It should be both of us suffering or both of us free—not this half-measure where I get to sip lattes with friends while my sister remains in Jax's clutches. Every moment of normalcy I steal feels like a betrayal.

But I need this. These slivers of ordinary life keep me from collapsing under the weight of everything else. They remind me of what we're fighting to get back to.

Still, as Daisy laughs at something Grace says, I can't help but wonder how Liv is coping.

24

EPILOGUE

AURORA

Six weeks later...

The elevator doors slide open to the penthouse, and I freeze. Every surface glimmers with candlelight, dozens of flames dancing across the space Hunter and I have shared these past desperate weeks. The dining table—usually covered with maps and surveillance printouts—is now draped in crisp linen, set with fine china and crystal glasses that catch the light.

"Hunter?" I call, setting my purse down. The scent of something delicious hangs in the air, a stark contrast to our usual hastily-prepared meals grabbed between search updates.

He appears from the kitchen, sleeves rolled up, looking more relaxed than I've seen him in days. "Welcome home."

"What's all this?" I gesture to the transformation around me. Six weeks of frantic searching, six weeks of dead ends and disappointments have worn us both down. This feels surreal, like stepping into someone else's life.

Hunter crosses to me, takes my hands in his. "I wanted

to do something nice for you. You've been so strong through all of this."

"But Liv—"

"Is still our priority," he assures me, brushing hair from my face. "But watching you check your phone every two minutes during dinner last night with your friends reminded me that we need moments to breathe too."

I hadn't realized he'd noticed my distraction during dinner. My friends had practically forced us out, insisting I needed a break from the penthouse and our constant search.

"You've barely slept. Barely eaten." His thumb traces my cheekbone. "I know how much you're hurting, how worried you are about Liv."

I lean into his touch, exhaling. "Any news?"

"Grayson's team found something promising in Colorado. It's early, but…" He hesitates. "I think we're getting close."

Hope flutters dangerously in my chest. We've had promising leads before.

"Tonight is just for us," Hunter continues, leading me toward the table. "Tomorrow we will keep fighting. But right now, I need you to sit down and let me take care of you for one evening."

Hunter serves roasted lamb with rosemary potatoes, and I can't help but be impressed. "You made this yourself?"

"Don't sound so shocked." He smirks, pouring red wine into my glass. "I've always been capable in the kitchen. I just rarely have a reason to show off."

We eat in silence for a few minutes, but something feels off. Hunter keeps glancing at me, then away. His knee bounces beneath the table, a nervous tic I've never seen from him before. Hunter Reed—always in control, always three steps ahead—seems... anxious.

"Are you okay?" I finally ask, setting down my fork. "You seem distracted."

He takes a deep breath, something unreadable crossing his face. "I've been thinking about what Jax took from us. The time. The trust. Almost you."

"Hunter—"

He pushes back his chair abruptly and moves to my side of the table. My heart stutters when he drops to one knee beside me—not like before when he begged forgiveness, but with clear purpose.

"This isn't how I envisioned this moment," he says, voice rough with emotion. "Before everything happened, I wanted to do this properly. Somewhere special, with everything perfect." His hand slips into his pocket, emerging with a small velvet box. "But if I've learned anything these past weeks, it's that we don't have the luxury of waiting for perfect moments."

He opens the box, revealing a simple solitaire diamond set in platinum. Beautiful in its understated elegance.

"Almost losing you..." His voice cracks, and he clears his throat. "When Jax took you, I realized I'd spent my entire life not caring about anyone but myself. Then suddenly, the thought of a world without you in it was unbearable."

Tears blur my vision as he takes the ring from its box.

"Aurora Harrison, I know we still have battles ahead of us. I know we're both broken in ways that may never fully heal. But I never want to be without you again. Will you marry me?"

My heart thunders in my chest as I look at the ring, then back to Hunter's face. Despite everything, I know my answer with absolute certainty.

"Yes," I whisper, then louder, "Yes, I'll marry you."

Hunter's hands tremble slightly as he slides the ring onto my finger. He pulls me into his arms, and I cling to him, this dangerous man who somehow became my safe harbor in the storm.

"I love you," I murmur against his neck.

He cradles my face, thumbs brushing away tears I hadn't realized were falling. "I love you too. More than I thought possible."

His kiss is so painfully gentle, almost reverent. When we break apart, I stare at the diamond catching candlelight on my finger, feeling a bittersweet ache.

"I just wish Liv could be here," I say, my joy dimming as I think of my sister, still out there somewhere with a madman. "This should be a moment we share together."

Hunter tucks a strand of hair behind my ear. "We're going to find her. Grayson said he thinks they're really close to closing in on their location. And when we do, we'll celebrate properly. All of us together."

I lean into his touch, trying to hold onto this moment of happiness amid our ongoing nightmare. "Remember when we told Derek about us?"

Hunter's mouth quirks. "How could I forget? I thought he might actually try to shoot me."

One week after returning to the city, we'd sat Derek down in his study. The thunderous expression on my stepfather's face when Hunter explained that the engagement to Liv was over and he was in love with me instead—I'd almost lost my nerve.

"He wasn't happy," I say, the understatement of the century.

"No, but he came around. Especially after learning Liv was involved with Ari."

I nod, remembering Derek's grudging acceptance. "He said he couldn't blame just you when clearly both Harrison women have questionable taste in men."

Hunter kisses me again. "We'll add finding your sister to our wedding to-do list, right at the top. And we won't be planning a wedding until she's back and safe. Let me get the champagne." He retreats to the kitchen and returns with a bottle of Dom Pérignon, the cork popping with a satisfying sound that makes me laugh. He fills two flutes, the bubbles catching the candlelight like tiny stars.

"To us," he says, clinking his glass against mine. "To the future Mrs. Reed."

The champagne is crisp and perfect. I set my glass down and move into his arms, still adjusting to the weight of the ring on my finger. "I never thought I'd feel this happy in the middle of everything else."

Hunter's eyes darken as he looks down at me. "I want to celebrate properly," he murmurs, his voice dropping to that low register that sends heat cascading through my body. His lips brush my ear. "I want all of you tonight. Every part I haven't claimed yet."

My breath catches at his meaning. "You mean...?"

"I want to pop that perfect little anal cherry of yours," he confirms, his bluntness making me blush despite everything we've already done together. "Tell me you'll let me have that tonight."

I've never done that before, though Hunter has hinted at it. Something about being engaged makes me brave. "Yes," I whisper, surprising myself with how much I want this new intimacy.

He lifts me, carrying me toward the bedroom. "I'll make it good for you," he promises against my neck. "I'll make you feel things you never imagined."

In the bedroom, Hunter takes his time undressing me, dropping kisses on each newly exposed patch of skin. I'm trembling by the time he lays me on the bed.

"On your hands and knees," he commands, and I comply, hearing him retrieve something from the nightstand drawer. "I've been thinking about this," he admits, his hands caressing my back. "Claiming every part of you."

I gasp as cool liquid drips where I've never been touched. Hunter's fingers are gentle but insistent, preparing me with patience. "Relax," he murmurs. "Trust me."

"I do," I breathe, meaning it completely despite our complicated past.

The cool sensation of lube makes me flinch, but Hunter's steady hand on my lower back keeps me in place.

"Relax, baby," he murmurs. "I'll make this good for you."

I try to breathe deeply as his slick finger circles where I've never been touched before, teasing and testing.

"That's it," he encourages as I consciously release the tension in my body. "Trust me."

His finger presses forward, entering me. The sensation is foreign and a little uncomfortable. While his one finger eases me open, his other slides beneath me, fingers finding my already sensitive clit.

"Hunter," I gasp, my hips jerking.

"Feel good?" He works a slow circle around my clit while his finger continues its gentle invasion.

Words fail me as pleasure builds from his skilled touch between my legs, distracting me from the unfamiliar pressure behind. When he adds a second lubricated finger, I barely register the burn before it transforms into a deep, pulsing pleasure.

"You're opening up so beautifully for me," Hunter praises, his fingers working in tandem—one hand bringing intense, familiar pleasure while the other introduces me to something entirely new.

The combination is overwhelming. My breathing turns ragged as he increases the pressure on my clit, circling faster while his fingers push deeper into my ass. The sensation builds, a different kind of orgasm forming—fuller, deeper somehow.

"Hunter, I'm—" I can't finish the sentence before waves of pleasure crash through me, my body clenching around his invasive fingers as I come with shocking intensity.

"Good girl," he whispers, continuing the gentle movements until the aftershocks subside.

Instead of feeling satisfied, the orgasm has only heightened my sensitivity, made me want more. The feeling of his fingers inside me—so foreign minutes ago—now feels necessary, like something I've been missing.

"More," I plead. "Please, I need more."

His fingers withdraw, only to return with a third digit stretching me further. The pressure increases—a delicious burn that makes me gasp and clutch at the sheets. Hunter works patiently, his free hand stroking my back, murmuring encouragement as my body yields to this new invasion.

"Almost there," he whispers, adding a fourth finger, stretching me to my limit.

The fullness is overwhelming now, beyond anything I've experienced. Just as I'm adjusting to the sensation, he slowly withdraws his fingers completely, leaving me empty and aching.

"What are you—" I begin, looking back over my shoulder.

My words die as I feel something larger pressing against my stretched opening—the blunt, thick head of his cock. Hunter drizzles more cool lube, massaging it around the sensitive rim.

"Ready?" he asks, gripping my hips to hold me steady.

"Yes," I breathe, wanting this final surrender.

Hunter pushes forward with careful pressure. For a moment, my body resists, but I force myself to relax, breathing deeply. The initial penetration sends a sharp jolt through me—pleasure mingled with discomfort—but I focus on accepting him, on opening myself completely.

"That's it," he encourages as my body yields, allowing his cock inside my ass.

The pressure is overwhelming as Hunter sinks deeper. I gasp, my fingers clutching the sheets.

"Fuck, Aurora," Hunter groans behind me. "Your ass feels so fucking good around me. So tight."

The fullness is unlike anything I've experienced—a delicious intrusion that borders between pleasure and pain. Each slight movement sends shockwaves through me.

"It's so good," I manage to say. "So full... you're stretching me so much."

Hunter begins slow, measured thrusts, each careful movement opening me further. The initial discomfort dissolves into a deep, throbbing pleasure that spreads through my entire body.

My hand slides between my legs, finding my clit swollen and sensitive. "That's it, baby," Hunter encourages. "Touch yourself while I fuck this perfect ass."

I circle my fingers over my clit as Hunter increases his pace, my body adjusting to accommodate him. The dual sensation is mind-bending—my fingers bringing familiar pleasure while Hunter fills me in this new, forbidden way.

"I can't believe how perfect you feel," he says, his voice strained with restraint. "I want to fill this tight virgin hole with my cum. I want to watch it drip out of you after I'm done."

His words send a fresh wave of arousal through me. "Yes," I moan, pushing back against him. "Please... I want that too."

The sensations overwhelm me as Hunter's thrusts become more urgent, his fingers digging into my hips. My own fingers move frantically between my legs, building toward another climax as he fills me completely.

"I'm so close," I gasp, feeling the tension coiling tighter within me.

"That's it," Hunter groans behind me, his rhythm faltering as he approaches his own release. "My future wife is going to take a load of cum in her tight little virgin asshole."

His words push me over the edge. I cry out as pleasure crashes through me, more intense than before. Hunter thrusts deeply once more with a guttural moan, his body tensing as he pulses inside me.

"Fuck, Aurora," he pants, holding himself deep as he empties himself.

We collapse together onto the bed, both spent and breathing heavily. Hunter carefully withdraws, pulling me against his chest. The diamond on my finger catches the light as I reach up to touch his face.

"Let's hit the shower," Hunter murmurs after a few minutes, pressing a kiss to my temple.

Under the warm spray, we kiss lazily, our hands exploring each other with unhurried appreciation. I wash his chest, tracing the scars that tell stories of his violent past. He returns the favor, his touch reverent as he glides soapy hands over my body.

"How does it feel?" Hunter asks, lifting my hand to examine the ring. "To be engaged to the most dangerous man in the city?"

I smile, watching water droplets cling to his eyelashes. "Surprisingly right."

He pulls me closer, his forehead resting against mine. "We're going to find Olivia. And when we do, nothing will be able to stop us."

I believe him. Despite everything we've been through—the lies, the revelations about my father, our separation—I trust in this love we've built. Whatever challenges lie ahead with Jax, whatever darkness we still need to face, I know our bond will hold.

"I love you," I whisper against his lips.

His eyes, usually so guarded, shine with emotion. "And I love you, future Mrs. Reed."

Thank you for reading Vow of Venom, the second book in the Hunter & Prey Duet. I hope you enjoyed Hunter & Aurora's story. What's next? If you want to find out what happened to Liv & Ari, I have a trilogy planned for their story, a why-choose MMF romance.

Oath of Deceit: A Dark Captive Mafia Romance

I'VE ALWAYS PLAYED the game of power and control. But when it comes to Liv, the stakes change.

She's the light in my dark world, the only one who can unravel my twisted heart.

My obsession with her is unquenchable, an addiction I can't escape.

But now, she's more than a desire; she's mine to possess.

When Ari comes in like a white knight to save her, I see an opportunity.

Strong, confident, and maddeningly attractive, I've always wanted him.

Now, he's my prisoner too, caught in my web of seduction.

Together, they will learn that in my world, there are no limits—only pleasure and pain intertwined.

I relish the power I hold over both of them, finding a dark thrill in domination.

The lines blur as I take on the role of their master, guiding them on a journey of exploration and surrender.

But Liv's feelings for Ari complicate the dance, igniting a wildfire of jealousy that threatens to consume us all.

They think they have a plan to escape my grasp, but they don't know the extent of my possessiveness—or the lengths I'll go to ensure they remain mine.

In this deadly game of deceit, desire, and twisted affection, I'm prepared to wield my power in every way imaginable.

In the end, why choose when you can have it all—all three of us bound together in a web of sin?

ALSO BY BIANCA COLE

Beautiful Monsters Series

Stalk Me: A Dark Mafia Romance

Shatter Me: A Dark Mafia Romance

Chain Me: A Dark Captive Mafia Romance

Hunt Me: A Dark Mafia Romance

Once Upon a Villain

Pride: A Dark Arranged Marriage Romance

Hook: A Dark Forced Marriage Romance

Wicked: A Dark Forbidden Mafia Romance

Unhinged: A Dark Captive Cartel Romance

Beast: A Dark Billionaire Romance

Wolf: A Dark Primal Mafia Romance

The Syndicate Academy

Sinister Games: A Dark Forbidden Mafia Academy Romance

Cruel Bully: A Dark Mafia Academy Romance

Sinful Lessons: A Dark Forbidden Mafia Academy Romance

Twisted Games: A Dark Enemies to Lovers Forbidden Mafia Academy Romance

Chicago Mafia Dons

Cruel Savior: A Dark Forbidden Mafia Romance

Violent Leader: A Dark Enemies to Lovers Captive Mafia Romance

Evil Prince: A Dark Arranged Marriage Romance

Brutal Daddy: A Dark Captive Mafia Romance

Cruel Vows: A Dark Forced Marriage Mafia Romance

Dirty Secret: A Dark Enemies to Lovers Mafia Romance

Dark Crown: A Dark Arranged Marriage Romance

Boston Mafia Dons Series

Empire of Carnage: A Dark Captive Mafia Romance

Cruel Obsession: A Dark Mafia Arranged Marriage Romance

Savage Bidder: A Dark Captive Mafia Romance

Ruthless King: A Dark Forbidden Mafia Romance

Vicious Bond: A Dark Brother's Best Friend Mafia Romance

Wicked Captor: A Dark Captive Mafia Romance

New York Mafia DonsSeries

Her Irish Daddy: A Dark Mafia Romance

Her Russian Daddy: A Dark Mafia Romance

Her Italian Daddy: A Dark Mafia Romance

Her Cartel Daddy: A Dark Mafia Romance

Romano Mafia Brother's Series

Her Mafia Daddy: A Dark Daddy Romance

Her Mafia Boss: A Dark Romance

Her Mafia King: A Dark Romance

New York Brotherhood Series

Bought: A Dark Mafia Romance

Captured: A Dark Mafia Romance

Claimed: A Dark Mafia Romance

Bound: A Dark Mafia Romance

Taken: A Dark Mafia Romance

Forbidden Desires Series

Bryson: An Enemies to Lovers Office Romance

Logan: A First Time Professor And Student Romance

Ryder: An Enemies to Lovers Office Romance

Dr. Fox: A Forbidden Romance

Royally Mated Series

Her Faerie King: A Faerie Royalty Paranormal Romance

Her Alpha King: A Royal Wolf Shifter Paranormal Romance

Her Dragon King: A Dragon Shifter Paranormal Romance

Her Vampire King: A Dark Vampire Romance

MY DARKER PEN NAME
SELENA WINTERS

I also write dark masked men romance, these books are typically darker than my mafia romances.

Hollow's Hunt

Unmasking Darkness: A Dark Romance

Kindred Kings: A Dark MM Romance

Double Trouble: A Dark Romance

Blackwood Brothers

Haunted: A Dark Primal Romance

Doomed: A Dark Primal Romance

Cursed: A Dark Primal Romance

Stalked: A Dark Primal Romance

Carnival Series

Carnival Nightmare: A Dark Stalker Romance

Carnival Obsession: A Dark Stalker Romance

Carnival Monster: A Dark Serial Killer Romance

Carnival Stalker: A Dark Stalker Romance

Carnival Master: A Dark Romance

Carnival Mayhem: A Dark Romance

Carnival Shadows: A Dark Stalker Romance

Convicts Series

Stranded: A Dark Romance novella

Salvation: A Dark Stalker Romance

Carjacked: A Dark Hitchhiker Romance

Hunted: A Dark Romance

Imprisoned: A Dark Prison Romance

Standalones

Game Over: A Dark Stalker Romance

Forbidden Harvest: A Dark Taboo Romance

Grave Intentions: A Dark Taboo Romance

Silent Stalker: A Dark Serial Killer Romance

My Bloody Valentine: A Dark Serial Killer Romance

Welcome to Carnage: A Dark Romance Novella

ABOUT THE AUTHOR

I love to write stories about over the top alpha bad boys who have heart beneath it all, fiery heroines, and happily-ever-after endings with heart and heat. My stories have twists and turns that will keep you flipping the pages and heat to set your Kindle on fire.

For as long as I can remember, I've been a sucker for a good romance story. I've always loved to read. Suddenly, I realized why not combine my love of two things, books and romance?

My love of writing has grown over the past four years, and I now publish exclusively on Amazon, weaving stories about dirty mafia bad boys and the women they fall head over heels for.

If you enjoyed this book, please follow me on Amazon, Bookbub, or any of the below social media platforms for alerts when more books are released.

Printed in Dunstable, United Kingdom